Steal Away Home

Steal Away Home

LOIS RUBY

Macmillan Publishing Company   New York

Maxwell Macmillan Canada   Toronto

Maxwell Macmillan International
New York   Oxford   Singapore   Sydney

Macmillan Publishing Company, 866 Third Avenue, New York, NY 10022
Maxwell Macmillan Canada, Inc., 1200 Eglinton Avenue East, Suite 200, Don Mills,
Ontario M3C 3N1
First edition
Printed in the United States of America

10 9 8 7 6 5 4 3 2 1

The text of this book is set in 12 point Berkeley Oldstyle Book.

Library of Congress Cataloging-in-Publication Data
Ruby, Lois.
Steal away Home / by Lois Ruby.
        p.   cm.
Summary: In two parallel stories, a Quaker family in Kansas in the late 1850s operates a
station on the Underground Railroad, while almost 150 years later, twelve-year-old Dana
moves into the same house and finds the skeleton of a black woman who helped the
Quakers.
ISBN 0-02-777883-5
[1. Fugitive slaves—Fiction. 2. Slavery—Fiction. 3. Underground railroad—Fiction. 4.
Quakers—Fiction. 5. Kansas— Fiction.] I. Title.
PZ7.R8314St   1994
[Fic]—dc20   93-47300

For Tom
who gets me where I need to be
and is always there with me

Contents

Steal Away Home

How will we know it's us without our past?

—John Steinbeck

CHAPTER ONE

Tear Down the Wall

If you'd asked that morning what Dana's chances were of finding a dead body before the day was out, she'd have said, "Well, it's never happened once in twelve and a half years, but you can always hope."

The hot wind was blowing cottonwood puffs through the open window. As Dana peeled red-and-white flock off the wall, she sucked a cotton puff into her nose and sneezed all over the wallpaper. Ripping away a damp strip, she found more of those awful orange roosters.

"Ohhh," she groaned, sinking back on her heels. How many more layers of ugly paper were there under this wall? Inches' worth, no doubt, for the 135 years the house had sat here on Tennessee Street.

The job was definitely worth more than seventy-five cents an hour, even if that's the best she could expect to make on a Saturday afternoon. Well, she'd go on strike.

She'd demand a raise, or a cushier job. But first she'd positively throw up at the sight of one more room full of roosters.

"Dana?" It was her mom's voice, in that frantic way she had of calling as though Dana had suddenly fallen into a well, or a robber were standing in the kitchen with panty hose over his head. "Dana! Where are you?"

"Here, Mom." She heard her mother's Birkenstock sandals flapping up the stairs.

More roosters. No chickens were pretty, but Dana hated these specimens most of all because of their color. Rusty orange, like her own hair, like her freckles. Everyone made fun of redheads, except for grandmothers, of course, who said the hair was *gorgeous,* who said the freckles were *adorable.* Well, there was nothing gorgeous or adorable about them, and nothing gorgeous or adorable about roosters, either.

And under the roosters, she'd probably turn up snapdragons, brown and gray, of course, because no one who'd lived in the nineteenth century had any eye for color.

"Dana Shannon, where in this huge barn are you?"

"Second floor, Mom, in the ugliest room in the house." It had a bristly maroon carpet, and odd angles that gave the room a Seven Dwarfs sort of look, and dim lights that made it seem like a murky puddle.

Her mom filled the door, her thin piano legs supporting her round body. She was like a bowling pin, turned upside down. A floppy shirt came to her knees, and sticking out of her sandals were padded feet with bright red nails. "Aren't we having fun? Or do blonds have more fun?"

"Redheads sure don't. Look at the wall."

"Oh Dana, tell me it's not more of them." She pulled away a swatch of red and white. "Oh no, roosters. I call fowl play." It's true, they'd found roosters behind nearly every wall's top layer, all over the house. There must have been a huge closeout on rooster paper, back when most people just had unfinished wood walls, and wallpaper was a rich man's luxury.

"Why did we ever buy this place, Mom, really?"

"Oh, your father's a romantic. He says it has historical importance, one of the first houses here in Lawrence, and all that. It's going to turn into the most terrific bed-and-breakfast in Kansas. Someday," she added, with a sigh. She ripped a strip of paper clear down the wall. It started out fat, then thinned like a stream of syrup. "I suppose I'll have to break down and rent a steamer."

Well yes, because it would take two lifetimes to get this paper off, and what for? Just for redheaded male chickens.

So Dana was devising a scheme to cut down on the work, even *with* a steamer, or else the spring and summer would fly by like a flock of hummingbirds, and she'd be left with the droppings. It was already about ninety degrees, with two more weeks till school let out. "I've got an idea, Mom. Why can't I take some sharp pointy thing and stab through eighty layers of this stuff? Then we can yank it off in chunks."

"Has its merits." Mom was on her hands and knees

3

ripping up a corner of the carpet that looked like one big wine stain. "Look at this gorgeous hardwood floor. Why would they cover it up? Oh, it's going to be a horrendously awful job refinishing this floor." Mom blew hair off her forehead. "First thing in the morning, I'm going to Bermuda."

"It's hot there, too."

"Anchorage, then."

Dana chipped away at a circle of the wallpaper with a carpet cutter, until the wall grew less spongy. The knife clunked against something hard. She turned the knife like a screwdriver and bored a little hole through the layers of paper. She worked it around and around, making the circle even wider, until she'd ground out a peephole the size of a walnut.

There behind the flock, the roosters, the snapdragons, and probably a few layers of zinnias and fleur-de-lis, was a wall of hard wood that absorbed the stab of her knife. And behind that, darkness.

Dana cut a wider hole. Now it was wide enough for a mouse, now for a squirrel. Pretty soon a good-sized cocker spaniel could have lodged himself in this cavity, like in a tree trunk. Dana peered into the hole. The darkness back there was impenetrable. She stuck her hand into the hole and pushed on the cool wood to get some idea how thick it was.

Suddenly it gave, it swung back. She poked her head into the cavern and smelled something old, musty. "Mom, the flashlight, quick!"

Mom scooted across the floor with the flashlight.

Behind the wall was a small room, and in the eerie shadows thrown by the thin light of the Eveready was a small crock, two cots, and on one of them—

A full skeleton.

CHAPTER TWO

No Names

April 1856

If he put his mind to it, he'd hear coyotes, but who wanted to? James whittled a stick into nothing but a fine thin point, the shavings growing into a billowy pile at his feet.

"James, pick up thy wood curls and wash up for dinner, son." His mother's long skirt swished as she spun around from her cookstove. "It's rabbit stew, lots of potatoes and carrots."

"When's Pa due back?" Dinnertime was always jollier when Pa was at the table. James noticed a slight hesitation before Ma spoke.

"Government business, as usual, James. Thy father's in Topeka with Dr. Robinson. He'll be back just before First Day, to be sure."

James went outside to wash his hands in a tub behind

the house. He'd lived the first twelve years of his life in Boston, but he'd be having his next birthday cake here in Kansas, in this shaky frame house, four city blocks distance from the nearest neighbor. There were terrors out here on the prairie. He was afraid of so many things that he wouldn't even tell his father about. Sometimes he told his sister, Rebecca, about how jittery he got when the wind whistled through the cracks in the roof, but then she got scared and cried, and he felt like a bully.

The wash water was gray and cold. He wiped his hands on a rag that hung above the washtub. It was as dark as pitch, barely a star in view. And where was the moon? Four blocks off he saw the pinpoint of light from a lantern in Macons' house. Jeremy Macon was probably doing his sums by that light. Jeremy Macon always had the right answer. Jeremy Macon was the kind who always got the girl. Not that James was interested in girls. Much.

The coyotes were hungry, howling like the wind in the trees. No telling what they'd eat if they got hungry enough. Jeremy and them, they hunted coyotes, and squirrels, too, and wild turkeys—anything that ran so fast that it was game enough to shoot. But James's father didn't keep a gun. He'd said, "Remember, my boy, we Quakers don't kill for sport. In fact, we don't kill any living things."

Lawrence was so blamed quiet, after the hustle and bustle of Boston. You couldn't hear a thing, except for the coyotes and the rustling brush. And then James thought he heard the grinding of wagon wheels in the dry dirt, over on the other side of the hill. Maybe not. Maybe it was the prairie wind playing tricks on him again.

What if a coyote came close? He balled his fists over his eyes. If only Pa would get back by dark every night.

They didn't kill living things, no, but they sure ate dead ones, and inside there was a tangy hot stew waiting for James, and inside there were no coyotes.

Ma and Rebecca were already at the table, their heads bowed. He slid onto the bench and tried to pray. Silence filled every crack of the dining room. Rebecca looked up at him and rolled her eyes. He'd burst out laughing! No! Ma would glare at him, and there'd be no gooseberry pie on his plate, come dessert time.

Finally, in some mysterious way, Ma knew it was time to stop praying. "James, thee dawdled outside. Was there something that caught thy eye?"

"My ear. I think someone's coming."

"Company!" Rebecca shrieked. She was five and loved when people came, because they usually brought her some sort of jimcrack or a string toy, or at least wild berry muffins for the whole family.

"Did thee see anyone?" Ma asked. She'd stopped eating and had scraped her stew back into the serving bowl.

"Grass is too tall," James said. Well, he'd eat his share *and* hers. And then it was unmistakable, the sound of wagon wheels. Ma's face got tight, and after a deep breath, a sort of peace came over it. "I expect we'll have guests for the night," she said. "Rebecca, finish thy meal quickly and go up and take thy pillow and feather quilt into thy brother's room."

"Aw, Ma. He stinks so bad."

"Do as I say, child."

The clattering of the wagon stopped out back of the house. There was a faint tapping at the window, and Ma lifted the corner of the curtain. "James, open the door, son, and be hospitable."

On the porch stood the shabbiest man James had ever seen, as if he'd ridden over dusty roads for days and weeks without a wash. His eyes were ringed with black, his face leathery. He had a finger missing, and James wondered where, how? Ma was right behind James now, craning to see beyond the driver.

"Evening, ma'am. Saw yer flag down out front. I've got cargo."

"Yes. Thee's welcome. James, give the man a hand."

James scrambled onto the wagon, wondering what the cargo was. The wonderful smell of smoke-cured ham made him swoon. He picked up the ham, wrapped loosely in rags, and pulled it to his face. Ohhh! Maybe the man was bringing them a winter's worth of fine Boston foods—meats that weren't like boot leather, or stringy as prairie chicken, or gamey as jackrabbit. "Smell's mighty good," James said.

"To cut the scent," the man muttered.

"Of what?"

"Negroes."

He'd heard of them, but had never seen one right up close. He and the driver pawed through layers of dishes, pots and pans, tools, and straw, until they came to a buffalo-hide blanket. The driver pulled that back, and James jumped. There on the floor of the wagon lay three of the blackest people on earth: A man, a woman, and a small boy with huge eyes, mostly whites.

"Y'all can come out," the driver said. "This here's Weavers' place."

The black man rose stiffly to his knees and pulled the woman up with both hands. The boy clung to his mother's thin dress as she stumbled to her feet. They were stiff as rakes. Lord knows how long they'd been lying on that bed of the wagon, flat as trampled prairie grass.

"Yep, this is Lawrence, Kansas, free soil. Y'all be safe here. Mind if I water my horse before I set out?"

He was already leading the mangy horse to the trough. Looked like it needed a night in a barn. But as soon as the horse lifted its head, the driver pulled it around toward the road again. "Well, I'm on my way." Where? James wondered. Where'd he come from, where was he going?

Now the Negro family huddled together, getting their land legs. They hadn't said a word. And what was James to do? Did they even speak English? He led them around the house to the front door. The wagon was already clattering back toward the hill.

"Ma!" Ma came to the door, Rebecca hiding behind her.

"Come in, friends," Ma said. "Thee's safe here. I've a hot supper for thee, and thee and thy child shall sleep in my daughter's bed tonight. After supper, my son will fetch water in our kettles, and we'll fill a hot tub for thee. Thee looks like a bath might be welcome."

"Thank you, ma'am. I'm Isaac—"

"Hush! No names."

"Yes'm."

"Tomorrow night just at dark, we'll send thee on. If I don't know thy names, why, I can't say for sure thee'd been here, anyone comes asking." She put ladles of stew on the tin plates and dark bread already thick with melted butter. The gooseberry pie would have to go a lot further, James thought mournfully.

But what he didn't know was that these were the first of many runaway slaves that would arrive in the dead of night. Ma would harbor them for a day of rest and hearty food, before she passed the fugitives on along the Underground Railroad—which wasn't a railroad at all.

And Ma told him that when this family of no-names got across the border into Canada, like so many others that went before them and that followed them, they'd sing:

> Oh, go an' carry de news,
> One more soul got safe!

But the runaways would only come to James's house when his pa was away on government business.

CHAPTER THREE

Identity: Unknown

"A *what*?" Dana's mom cried. "Let me have a look." Dana held the flashlight for her. "Oh my God, it *is* a skeleton. Dana, call 911."

"Me? You're the adult here."

Her mother backed away. "Well, it's not going anywhere, I suppose. I mean, there's time to do this civilly. Come on. We'll go downstairs to the phone. We'll dial 911, and we'll calmly tell them that there's a complete skeleton in a secret compartment of our upstairs parlor. Smiling broadly. Empty eye sockets just staring right at us. Oh Dana, they'll send the men in the white coats for us, with big butterfly nets."

Dana's mom talked too fast when she was nervous, and her fingers flew like buzzing bees. Dana was just the opposite. She clamped shut, like an oyster shell, rolling all the scary things around in her head.

The police came quickly, maybe because Mrs. Shannon's call had been a little different from the usual run of intruders and domestic spats. A skeleton, indeed!

A guy who looked more like an accountant than a policeman introduced himself as Officer Burney. "This is my partner, Officer Wyles," he said, and both flashed IDs. Wyles was the first woman police officer Dana had ever talked to. She seemed so small and delicate. Dana couldn't imagine her pulling a revolver on a thug, or throwing a robber over her shoulder in a swift karate maneuver. But Wyles had intense eyes. Maybe she stopped crooks with her laser vision.

Each of the police officers peered into the secret chamber behind the wall and didn't seem at all startled, as if they found perfect anatomy-class specimens every day. But Officer Burney called down to headquarters for help. Before long, a photographer was there, and fingerprinters, and a work crew to tear down the wall.

"One way to get the work done quick," Dana said. "Maybe we can get them to rip up the carpet, too."

Then, here came Dr. Baxi, who was the county coroner.

"Oh Punir, I'm so glad to see you!" Dana's mom nearly crushed the little man in her enthusiasm. "This is a B-grade movie. Unbelievable. Something out of the annals of Scotland Yard."

Dr. Baxi gave her his shy smile, but was all business. "Don't move the remains," he said, in his clipped Indian way, as two policemen were trying to figure out how to haul the body away. He showed the photographer which angles to shoot from, had him standing up on the cot, straddling the skeletal feet. As he jiggled the cot, Dana noticed that the bones were where they should be, but not all of them were attached, as though someone had found them and arranged them just so.

"How come he's not connected, Dr. Baxi?" asked Dana.

He pointed here, and here. "See, some ligaments still connect the bones."

"This is sick," her mother said, and she sank into a rocking chair. Officer Wyles had to step back and forth over her feet.

With rubber gloves, Dr. Baxi picked up scraps of faded fabric and dropped them tenderly into plastic bags, each one with a note describing where he'd found it. "Cotton," he said. "Very old."

"Val? Dana?" Her dad was running up the stairs. "Is everybody okay?" He paused at the door of the parlor. "Geez, it looks like a tornado hit." He elbowed his way through the crowd in the parlor and flung his arms around Dana and her mom, while he stared at the gaping hole in the wall. "Thank God you're okay. Now would somebody tell me what's going on here?"

"You won't believe this, Dad."

He stepped over the foot-high chunk of wall into the secret chamber. "Punir, what are you doing here? Oh," he said, backing out. His face was ashy white.

"Somebody's been dead a long, long time behind that wall, Dad."

"More than a hundred years," Dr. Baxi said. "That's an educated guess. Bones are clean, teeth are intact, there's still a tuft of hair on the back of the scalp." Dana leaned in for a closer look. Sure enough, there were a few wisps of black hair standing stiffly up from the skull.

Her father could barely get the words out. "Who is it? *Was* it?"

"We don't know yet," Dr. Baxi said, as he directed two men to slide a thin plank under the skeleton. He carefully held each bone just so. The men wrapped a tight canvas over the skeleton and tied it under the stretcher. "Hold it steady," Dr. Baxi directed them, as they stepped over the rubble in the room and took the very thin corpse out of the house. Dr. Baxi followed. "I will phone you later," he said somberly, and then as though cheered by this new thought, he motioned for the bearers to stop, and he said, "Dana, my wife tells me you are quite a biology buff." Mrs. Baxi was her Life Sciences teacher at Thoreau. "Maybe you would like to be present for the autopsy?"

"Would I!" Ever since her mother would let her hold a sharp knife, she'd dissected worms, fish, fish eyes, slabs of liver from the kitchen. Once, a bird had fallen out of a tree and been abandoned by its mother, and it came under Dana's knife. The red, stringy, spongy insides of a dead thing always seemed so much more, well, *alive.* "I'll be a big help, I promise."

"I don't mean present in the actual autopsy theater, but you could be just outside in my office."

"I won't faint, Dr. Baxi, honestly."

His smile made his small eyes vanish. "But there are laws, my dear. You shall be the first to get word when we complete our examination."

"All right," she said, disappointed. But it was better than nothing, and maybe when the door swung open, she could steal peeks of something gory to describe to her friends.

"I'll call you in the morning," Dr. Baxi promised. "I'll need this evening to get records prepared. Jeffrey, you know Simon Fleicher, the forensic anthropologist at the university. Do you know if he's in town? I'll call him in on the case also. Very intriguing," he said, snapping off his rubber gloves as he followed the stretcher down the stairs.

"We have a few questions, Dr. Shannon," Officer Wyles said, nailing him with her eyes. "A few preliminary questions before Homicide gets here."

"Homicide?" Dana's mother was having trouble processing all this. "Jeffrey? Is this in my contract?"

But Dr. Shannon wasn't doing much better. History was his field at the university, not criminology or anthropology. What did he know about murder investigations and identifying bones, especially bones that were a century old? Dana seemed to be the only one staying calm. *Good thing they won't be at the autopsy,* she thought.

She climbed back into the room for a last look, because the police would be sealing it off soon for their investigation. Everybody was talking at once, firing questions, answers, orders, theories. This was *not* the typical case. No one was in charge, and everyone was the boss. People passed back and forth from the secret chamber, carrying equipment in, carrying equipment out. Officer Wyles pulled out the cot so one of Dr. Baxi's men could lift fingerprints from the wall, and Dana thought she saw something drop down to the floor.

"You're not supposed to be in here," the coroner's man said, as he busied himself with his fingerprint kit.

Dana squatted and quickly picked up a small black book, which she slipped into the pocket of her jumper.

"And don't touch anything," the man said. "Leave it to the public to gum up every one of our investigations."

"I'm out of here," Dana said merrily. The black book slapped her thigh as she stepped over the open gash of the wall.

"Just in time." Officer Burney taped a crisscross of yellow plastic over the gaping hole, stamped with the message: DO NOT BREAK THIS SEAL, UNDER PENALTY OF LAW, BY ORDER OF THE LAWRENCE POLICE DEPARTMENT. Officer Wyles crossed that out and wrote in black marker: BY ORDER OF THE DOUGLAS COUNTY CORONER.

"Let's get out of here," Dana's father said, and the three of them drifted off to a guest bedroom. They sat on the floor with their backs up against the four-poster. Someday this room would rent for $120 a night, but not for a while, since people wouldn't be too excited about staying in a house where skeletons turned up.

"What do you think happened, Dad?"

"I have no idea. I've got the librarian hunting up some documents on the house already, so we'll know what we're doing as we restore it to its nineteenth-century state. They should have the materials by Monday. And I'll go down to the Douglas County Register of Deeds, see what I can find out about the previous owners of the house. But right now, who knows?"

Dana fingered the book in her pocket. It felt like an address book or a pocket calendar, but very heavy for its size. Should she show it to her parents? "Suppose somebody found something in that little room," she began.

"Like what?" Her mother sounded distant and disconnected, like a bad phone line. But her father was looking at her closely.

"Oh, I don't know. A little knickknack or something?"

"If I found something," her father said carefully, "I'd give it to the police right away, even though the historian in me would want to keep it and study it."

That's the way her parents were. They never said, "You have to do this, don't you dare do that." They always laid out the choices, let her know what they thought she should do, then made her decide. Her friends thought this was really cool, especially Ahn Thuey, whose Vietnamese family controlled every inch of her life. But Dana's friends didn't understand how hard it was to have the responsibility back on your own shoulders. If you blew it, you had no one to blame but yourself.

So, that settled it. She'd show them the black book—but not until she'd had a chance to find out just what was in it.

"I need to fix dinner," her mother said, "if they ever get out of our house. Or do we feed all the civil servants of Lawrence?"

Dana's dad said, "Let's go out and get a pizza. It'll be a long time before anything's settled."

As it turned out, it would be months before anything was settled, and even then, there were unsolved puzzles.

Half the police department of Lawrence gathered outside Dr. Baxi's lab. How often did they get a chance to investigate bones that were over a hundred years old? An assistant was issuing everyone masks, and Dana casually took one. "Now, you'll stand free and clear of the table. Don't get in the coroner's way. And keep your mouths shut, because he'll be dictating his findings and you don't want your witticisms to be preserved in the record for all eternity, right? People get in the autopsy room and think they have to make jokes. Believe me, we've heard them all." Dana tied the paper mask around her head and watched everyone else suck air in and out.

"And if you feel like you're going to faint, get out of the theater on the double. We don't want two stiffs on the table." This was obviously a line he'd delivered a thousand times, but still found hilarious.

They filed into the lab. It was cold, like a morgue. There were two other doctors besides Dr. Baxi, and Dana also recognized Dr. Fleicher, the forensic anthropologist from the university.

Dr. Baxi's eyes were fixed on the arrangement of bones on his table. A sheet covered all but the head and shoulders. "We will observe strict hygienic conditions," he announced. It seemed silly to worry about sanitary conditions, considering how dead the body was, but then Dana wondered if they might be worried about catching something from the skeleton.

Dana had to stand on her tiptoes and peer between the shoulders of the doctors and policemen. Twice she was elbowed in the ribs. The anthropologist reached under the sheet and lifted one bony hand lovingly, as if it were a dozen roses. One of the policemen swooned, stepped back, and tromped on Dana's foot.

"Ouch," she whispered, and Dr. Baxi looked up sharply, recognizing her. With a slight nod of his head and a rolling of his eyes, he motioned for her to leave.

How absolutely demoralizing, treating her just like a child.

"But—"

A policeman took her firmly by the arm and parked her in Dr. Baxi's office. He stripped off his mask and left, looking glad to be out of the lab himself. Hours passed, it seemed, or maybe thirty minutes, as Dana studied photos on the walls of horrible murder scenes and crashes. A skeleton hung in the corner, with its perpetual smile fixed on Dana. She gave it a poke, and it danced for her, bones clattering—a poor substitute for the *real* bones inside the lab.

Finally, an assistant came for her and took her back into the lab. Everyone was gone, but Dr. Baxi gave Dana a private briefing.

"This is what we know," he said. "The subject is five feet three inches and is female, which we can tell by the breadth of the pelvic bone, but more clearly by the smoothness of the back of the skull. Later, this will be confirmed through DNA analysis of the tooth enamel. Excellent teeth, by the way. She has all of them. And see here how the eye sockets are shaped, and the nose?"

Dana studied the skull carefully. It looked like every skull she'd ever seen on poison bottles, on Halloween skeletons, in books, in museums, in Dr. Baxi's office.

"We can tell by the eyes, the nose, and the hair that the woman was of the Negro race. Age, somewhere between eighteen and twenty-four. Difficult to say exactly. I can tell she's never given birth or broken any bones. Look at her, what do you think? Left-handed, or right-handed?"

"I don't know. Right, I guess," which she guessed because the odds were with her.

"Left-handed. See? The bones of the left arm are slightly longer. She worked very hard in her life. Look here at the spurs on her heels. Stress. Maybe she walked hundreds of miles."

"I wonder who she was," Dana said quietly.

"The forensic anthropologist may have a clearer idea when he completes his study. He may even be able to reconstruct her face. But here is my working hypothesis." Dr. Baxi held the Dictaphone tape up, as if she could read it. "I believe the subject was a fugitive slave who died 130 to 140 years ago. Her identity is unknown, and the cause of death is unknown. I'm recommending further investigation. Are you interested in pursuing it further? My wife says you have a fine scientific mind. You'll find some answers, my dear."

CHAPTER FOUR

The Wakarusa War

April 1856

James slept a little later the next morning. Rebecca had talked to him half the night, kicked the rest of the night, and there wasn't a minute he was covered with the blanket. Once she got up, he slept like a baby. But when he finally got downstairs, Rebecca and Ma and the Negro family were already half done with breakfast. The runaways were solemnly working their way through a stack of flapjacks. The boy ate with his hands; maple syrup streamed down his arms.

"Was thee sleeping away the day?" Ma asked, with a sparkle to her voice.

"It's barely sunrise," he replied. "Has thee even heard the cock crow yet?"

"I heard the stomachs growl," Ma said. "That was

enough to rouse me. Now, sit down before the flapjacks are cold as stone."

James noticed that Rebecca sat right up close to the boy, cutting his pork sausage into bite-sized bits like a little mother.

"Now," Ma said, putting a dainty bite into her mouth. *I'll catch her talking with her mouth full!* James thought, but no, she chewed slowly, and they all waited for her. "Now, without saying where thee's come from, tell us how long thee's been, shall we say, traveling."

"This is the fourth day, ma'am," the man answered, keeping his eyes on his plate.

James pictured the map on the wall in Miss Malone's classroom, imagining inches for miles, miles for days. They couldn't have come from Georgia or someplace in the Deep South. They'd be way out of their way here in the Kansas Territory. From Georgia, they'd have gone up through South Carolina, North Carolina, Virginia, Washington, Maryland, and into Pennsylvania, which was a free state. No one came this way, through the blamed wilderness. Reasonable people didn't even live here, James reminded himself.

Unless these Negroes came from Missouri. James had been hearing all about the scuffles between Missouri and Kansas over who had a right to hold slaves. Missouri was a slave state, and Kansas, which wasn't even a state yet, was still fighting it out. Of course, the settlers in Kansas Territory wanted to be Free-Soilers, and that's what they voted for. That's why Quaker families like James's settled in Kansas, instead of Missouri, or instead of continuing on west along the Oregon Trail.

23

But slaveholders in Missouri had a different plan. They swarmed across the border, which is why they were called Border Ruffians, and stuffed the ballot boxes and made it *look* like more Kansans were proslavery. At the last voting, one even shouted, "We are going to have Kansas if we wade to the knees in blood to get it."

The Lawrence Free-Soilers refused to accept the results of the voting that elected a proslavery legislature. They called it a bogus government, headed by Governor Shannon. Ma said, "Hmph, the man's nothing but a scoundrel." Now Pa was off in Topeka with other Kansas Territory men, trying to hammer out a constitution so Kansas could become a state, a *free* state. They were electing a Free-Soil legislature, and they were putting up their own Dr. Charles Robinson for governor. But it sure wasn't easy.

All last year, before James and his family had come from Boston, there'd been border skirmishes—the Wakarusa War, they were calling it, for the Wakarusa River that pulsed through Lawrence, and it wasn't over yet. A small civil war, they were calling it, because proslavery and antislavery people from the same Union fought each other at arm's length. They were close enough to see what color eyes the enemy had, smell his breath.

Jeremy Macon had told James all about it, about how he'd gotten to shoot one of those Sharps rifles. "James Weaver, it was so exciting. You missed it. Best thing that's happened in my lifetime."

Jeremy and he were walking into town, where they'd go to Miss Malone's class in Dr. Robinson's big house.

James kicked stones, while Jeremy rambled on and on about the rifles and the war and all. "Early in fifty-five, all these boxes came in on barges up the Kansas River. They were marked Books." Jeremy chuckled. "You'd have thought every man in Lawrence was a bookworm, by the number of books that landed here. Inside the boxes— Sharps rifles, the newest thing in repeating guns. My pa got one," Jeremy said proudly. " 'Course, your pa wouldn't have."

No, James thought, they would be sitting out the whole Wakarusa War, while his pa talked and talked long into the night with other Quaker men. All words and no action. "Pa," he'd said one night, "ever think about the man who said, 'Action speaks louder than words'?" Pa had given it a good two minutes' thought, in that Friends way of weighty, churning silence. "Well, son, here's what I believe. Words speak softer than actions. But there's nothing more powerful than the word, beginning with the Good Word of the Lord." Jeremy would have had a good laugh over that one.

"And you know what they called these rifles, James? Beecher's Bibles."

"No!"

"Truth." Jeremy crossed his heart. "Henry Ward Beecher, why he got up and spoke at the Congregational Church last year. Said we had to raise money for self-defense. Said get guns in here, not Bibles."

This was heresy. If James's parents could hear this—

"Said a rifle's a higher moral power so far as these proslavers are concerned. Said you might as well read the Bible to buffaloes as to one of them slaveholders. That's how come they're called Beecher's Bibles." Jeremy laughed raucously, then added, "Maybe *thee* wouldn't call 'em that, but *we* would!"

Now the runaways—probably from Missouri—sat at James's table and ate more flapjacks than he'd ever seen anyone pack away before, all of them washed down with creamy milk.

Ma said, "Best thee not go outside today. We don't know much about our neighbors yet."

So James wondered what they'd all do indoors—play chess?

But Ma had it all planned out. She turned to the young woman, who still hadn't said a single word. "Missus, I could use a hand with the ironing today. It's my day to wash bed linens. Oh, and James promised his pa he'd fix that sagging bed frame you slept on upstairs. He's a smart boy, but he's not an expert with a hammer and nails," Ma said, giving the man a chance to make the offer.

"I'm good with tools. Can fix most anything, ma'am."

"Fine. James, show him the toolbox. And Rebecca, take the boy down to the cellar. I want thee to count every jar down there. Does thee know thy numbers, child?" The all-eyes boy shook his head. "Well, but thee can tell tomatoes from corn. After they're sorted and counted, bring up a jar of each thing you find, and we'll send them off with these good people tonight." She clapped her hands. "Thee's still sitting?"

All of them scrambled to their feet. The woman gathered plates and cups and took them to the washbasin. Rebecca dragged the boy by the hand toward the cellar door. And James wondered how he'd do, alone with a Negro man for the first time. Would he give off a different scent? What if he couldn't think of a thing to say to the man, like he got sometimes with Bethany Maxwell.

Upstairs, the man riffled through the toolbox until he found four sturdy nails. Then he shoved up his threadbare sleeves and took the bed apart, looking at it every which way. He could stay squatted for the longest time without toppling.

James asked, "Can it be fixed?"

"Yessir."

Sir? It was the first time an adult had ever called him that! James watched him drive a nail into the wood with two fierce thwacks of the hammer. He handed the hammer to James to do the other side. James smacked his thumb a few times, but got the nail in good and straight, while he thought about how the bed ought not to need nails. It should be built so that each section fit perfectly, tightly into each other section. James imagined beautiful lumber sanded smooth as glass—not this nubby old cottonwood. And the bed he saw would be on four carved legs, high enough that it would take a footstool to climb up into bed. Then you'd sink into a feather mattress a foot thick. . . .

"Mr. James, sir?"

"Sorry, I was off somewhere else, I guess."

"Yessir, but you nailed your shirt to the bed."

James yanked at his shirt and heard a sickening rip. Ma would never let him hear the end of this, while she patched his shirt.

"Hold up, Mr. James." The man expertly separated the two pieces of wood so James could slide his shirt out.

"She's going to tan my hide." James quickly tucked the shirttail into his trousers.

The man snorted, fighting back laughter.

"Thee musn't tell my mother. Promise?"

"Yessir!"

At dusk that night, the runaways were layered in the warmest clothes Ma could find. The woman carried a cloth bundle over her shoulder—canned tomatoes and corn, dark bread, some jerky, the last wedge of gooseberry pie. They waited. Finally, a strange man came to the door, but Ma seemed to recognize him.

"I heard no wagon wheels," Ma said.

"Couldn't shake a wagon free, Miz Weaver. I'll walk 'em to the next station." James saw the woman's eyes plead with Ma.

"Thee's well in this man's hands," Ma assured them. She gathered them together, like ducks in the yard. "God go with thee," she said, tears in her eyes.

When they were gone, she turned hard and dry again. "James, Rebecca, thee's not to say a word of this to anyone."

"Not even to Pa?" Rebecca asked.

Ma shook her head. "And not to the neighbors, not to thy friends, thy teachers, no one."

"A secret!" Rebecca squealed.

"But Pa—" James began.

"Pa and I are of the same mind on this slavery business. He's doing it his way, I'm doing it mine. Swear." She reached for a Bible on the hutch behind her. "Come, Rebecca, thee, too, James."

All three placed their hands on the Bible. "I swear," James said, with a heavy chest.

CHAPTER FIVE

Night of the Living Bones

Of course, finding that secret chamber and the skeleton gave Dana's life a little more glamour. She became a local hero at Thoreau Middle School on Monday, when everyone was buzzing about the Night of the Living Bones.

"Who killed her?" kids at the lunch table wondered, and Mike Gruber acted like the chief detective on the case: "We've got to get to the bottom of this."

"Well, Mike, it's not like there's a killer running loose around Lawrence," Dana reminded him. "The girl's been dead about 135 years."

Ahn said, "She has a name, you know." She bit into her taco, and meat flew everywhere.

"You know her actual name?" Sally Benedetti asked.

"Of course," Ahn answered. "Because Dana and I named her. She's Elvira Lincoln."

So then the whole seventh grade was talking about

Elvira, with just a hint of awe, as though she were an eighth grader, someone ready to move into high school next year.

"Wasn't Elvira wearing any clothes?" Derek Boyles asked. "Not even underwear?"

"I guess it all rotted off of her, like her flesh," Dana explained. "They found a few scraps of cotton that looked like rags that have been through the washer about ten thousand times. And a little crock, and that's all." Not a word about the diary.

"It is so sad, so sad," Sally mused. "I mean, she died all alone in that room, no one to hold her hand."

Mike asked, "How do you know that? Maybe she was already dead, and someone dumped her in that room to hide the body. Maybe that's why they can't find any clothes. What do you think, Jeep?"

"Yeah, Jeep, you haven't said a word about Elvira," all the kids said.

Jeep Jeffreys slurped his canned peaches, while everyone waited for his reply.

"Speak to us, oh Prophet Jeep, we're hanging on every word."

Dana thought Jeep's dark skin looked pale and dusty today. Maybe it was his new haircut—no more square Afro; now his hair was cut right up close to his scalp. Or maybe he didn't like talking about dead bodies while he ate. They all stared at him a minute, until he shoved his tray across the table and said, "Get off my back."

"Hey, what's 'a matter?" Derek asked. "What did I do?"

"Not you, Derek, you're not the center of the uni-

31

verse," Mike reminded him. They watched Jeep dump his leftover green beans and stewed tomatoes in the trash and slide his tray onto the conveyer belt. "Hey, where ya going?" Mike yelled across the room.

Jeep came back to the table and straddled the bench. "Okay, this pile of bones, this Elvira? She was a slave, right? So how come you think that's so funny?"

"Sorry, man," they all murmured, but in another minute, they were bursting with more questions about Elvira—whether she was married, or dating anyone special, whether she'd been from a plantation in Georgia or Mississippi, whether she'd run off or been chased off, whether she'd died in the room, or been killed somewhere else and carried there.

"This is sick," Jeep muttered, and he went to the gym to shoot baskets.

Dana didn't even tell her best friend, Ahn, about the diary. On the Night of the Living Bones, the police and city people hadn't cleared out until ten o'clock. Then her parents were watching some 1930s movie downstairs; the black and white images flickered on the window opposite the TV.

"I'm going to bed," Dana said, forcing up a yawn. Upstairs she locked her door and finally had a chance to look at the small black book. The title page was yellowed, but the words were written in a tight, economical script, very black and straight:

NOTES FROM THE UNDERGROUND:
1856 TO ? by MILLICENT WEAVER

Dana turned to page one.

> April 25, 1856—The first ones have been here, and
> if Thou hast been with them, they are well on their
> way to Canada. The eyes of that puny little boy were
> enough to convince me that I'm doing what I must,
> though Mr. Weaver would rightly disapprove. In
> all my years of matrimony, I've not kept secrets
> from Caleb, but I believe I am answering Thy call.
> Please, shelter James and Rebecca, as we are shelter-
> ing the Negroes. Lord, what have we gotten our-
> selves into?

"Guys?" Dana's parents were enraptured by the shades of
black and white on the TV screen. Their robot arms
moved from popcorn bowl to mouth. "Mom? Dad?" Her
mother shoved the popcorn toward her, in an obvious
attempt to silence her. "If I tell you I found something,
you've got to promise to let me keep it, and you've got to
promise not to act like parents."

"It's not a lizard or a bat or anything, is it?"

"No, Mom." Dana grabbed the remote control and
zapped the TV off.

Her mother yelped, "Dana! It's Bette Davis in *Jezebel*."

"And this is Dana Shannon in *Keeping Evidence from the
Police*." That got their attention. "I found a diary in the
room."

"As I suspected," her father said. "Let me see it."

Dana shook her head. "It's hidden, so you can't make
me give it up—yet. Dr. Baxi said I should find some
answers about the bones. I think the journal of Millicent
Weaver will help."

Her mother said, "Honey, it's not right to—"

"Even if I can't solve the mystery, I'll turn the diary over to Dr. Baxi by July 1. Deal?"

Her parents exchanged glances and sealed their own pact. Finally, her father said, "It's more than a deal, Dana, it's your solemn word."

CHAPTER SIX

The Free-State Hotel

May 1856

"Pa, Pa!" Rebecca cried, trampling the new spring cro-
cuses by the front door. Her feet sank into fresh mud,
and she glanced back over her shoulder. "James, it's Pa!"

"Yes, I see." He hung back on the porch with Ma, who
was smoothing wisps of hair over her ears, sealing them
put with fingers of spit. Women!

Pa swung Rebecca around in a circle and gave James a
manly hug, but it was Ma his eyes lit on. "Millicent," he
whispered, his lips in her hair. They were as close as a
foot to a boot, and James knew why, now. Jeremy and them,
they'd discussed it all during the ten days Pa had been
gone. Now James's face felt flushed, and he looked away.

Rebecca tugged at Pa's coat. "Millicent, there's a pup

nipping at me. Has thee gone and brought a pup into the house?"

"It's me, Pa."

"Not a pup, Caleb. A prairie chicken. They wander in the house, just like that."

"It's me!" Rebecca cried.

"Hear it clucking, Mrs. Weaver?"

"Faintly, Mr. Weaver."

"Pa-a-a!"

He swooped Rebecca up in his arms again, scissored her on his hip, and had a good, hard look at James. "Son, are thy britches still reaching thy boots?"

"Sir?"

"Looks to me like thee's grown two inches since I've been gone."

Lately James had noticed there was barely enough shirttail to tuck into his pants. Now he quickly checked to make sure the nail rip wasn't showing.

"Eats like there's no tomorrow, Caleb. Thee should have seen him with his face in a gooseberry pie."

And that reminded Rebecca. "Oh Pa, we had company the night of the pie."

James saw his mother's eyes throw a warning, but Rebecca never looked her way to catch it. So James squeezed her heel. "Ouch!"

Pa set her down on the floor, and James sank to the floor beside her to grab hold of her arm if necessary.

"Company?" Pa said.

Back home company was nothing to make a speech about, but out here—

"Mrs. Macon came by," Ma said brightly. "Brought us

some bread-and-butter pickles. Just a bit too sweet, if you ask me." By now James had twisted Rebecca's arm far enough behind her that she remembered to shut her trap, and Ma deftly separated them.

"I'm right glad, Millicent, that thee's finally making friends with the local ladies."

Which told James just how lonely Ma must be out here.

Ma said, "But tell us, Caleb, do we have a state constitution?"

"Not yet," he said brusquely. "Four or five more months of haggling it out with words might do it. It's thorny, Mil, not an easy thing. Now, I'd like to go out back and wash up. Son, are thy hands caked with the sweat of thy labors?"

James looked at his hands. No need to wash too often, and he'd done no labor. But then he realized his pa meant to have a minute alone with him.

At the washtub, Pa asked, "Who really came by the house, James?"

James had never lied to his father; had kept a few things tucked inside his head, but had never out-and-out lied. "I've been busy with school, Pa, studying down at Macons' and all. I'm not here much."

His father cleaned dirt out from under his nails, then splashed cool water on his face. Beads of water clung to his beard, and he shook them off like a dog shakes off a bath. "Thee must watch after thy mother and sister when I'm away, son."

"Yes sir." James slapped a handful of water on his face.

"And take care thee doesn't wash off thy mustache, James."

37

* * *

After Rebecca went to bed, Ma rocked and knitted a summer bonnet for her, while James drew windows of every which shape and size. They talked about the constitution business again, and the newly elected legislature.

Pa filled every inch of his chair, with his legs stretched out in front of him and his heels digging into the clay floor. "Well, and it was a testy situation. Thee would have reeled, Millicent, if thee could have heard the deputy marshal announce that President Pierce intended for us all to be arrested if we took the oath of office."

James's heart lurched at the thought of Pa and Dr. Robinson and the others wallowing in some jail cell.

"Well," Ma said, "I surely hope a little threat like that didn't stop thee from doing what was right."

"A little threat, Mrs. Weaver? Franklin Pierce is president of the United States of America."

"And thee is a free man, Mr. Weaver, or thee wouldn't be here tonight telling us this tale."

"True," Pa said, deflated. "We took the oath of office. Had to, to be sure the free-state constitution would be recognized throughout the territory."

"Well, so it was a tempest in a teapot," Ma said, with a bit of play in her voice. James looked up from his drawing, watched her knit another round on the bonnet before she said, "I'm just as pleased not to be taking plum cake to the jailhouse, Caleb."

"I've heard talk of some trouble," Pa said. Ma's needles clicked in the pause. "They're saying the First U.S. District Court's about to hand down a decision."

There was Pa, talking like a lawyer again. "Decision about what, Pa?"

"Well, it has to do with abuses of the Fugitive Slave Law." Ma knitted faster, racing across each row now. "No matter what we think about slavery, it's illegal in this country to help slaves escape."

Ma tucked her needles under her arm. "Caleb Weaver, what they're doing to those Negroes is immoral."

"I wouldn't argue with you, Mrs. Weaver. I'm just saying there's a law, and the law says that, much as we want to see Kansas a free state—we're obliged to help slave owners get their property back."

"Property, indeed, Mr. Weaver!"

"In the legal sense."

"Oh, piffle."

Now the silence was hot and stingy, and James's voice cut a slice out of the thick air. "Pa, the Eldridge Brothers' Free-State Hotel's opening up next week, over on the corner of Massachusetts and Winthrop. I hear it's so big, they can stable fifty horses out back."

Pa said, "Why, I'm told they're already using the dining room as a barracks, stockpiling meat and such for the siege."

"Caleb," Ma warned, but he ignored her.

"General Lane's out there on the prairie, drilling soldiers for battle."

Ma rapped her knitting needles like drumsticks. "Caleb Weaver, thee musn't talk this way."

"Mrs. Weaver," Pa said firmly, "thee must ready thyself. Our neighbors are preparing for war."

Ma's face was furled with disapproval. In a voice barely above a whisper, she said, "Edna Macon and the other ladies are making cartridges out of lead and gunpowder smuggled in by their men. Doing this in their very kitchens."

Pa slid his rocking chair up to Ma's, and she looked him right in the eye as she quoted, " 'They shall beat their swords into plowshares, their spears into pruning hooks.' "

"And their rifles into Beecher's Bibles."

"James Baylor Weaver! Bite thy tongue!"

"Sorry, Ma." But he wasn't sorry. Every time he walked past Fort Necessity, the circular mud fortress at the foot of Massachusetts, and saw a sentinel of the Free State Army of Kansas Volunteers, James couldn't help but cock his ear to catch the first thrilling report of gunfire. He remembered Grampa Baylor once saying, "Well now, James, bear in mind that a Quaker never raises his hand in wrath against another man." "Yessir," James had murmured. And Grampa Baylor had fixed his filmy eye on James. "Neither does he roll over and play dead, son. Time comes, thee will know what to do."

Would he, if it came right down to it?

CHAPTER SEVEN

No Nancy Drews

Ahn slept over on Friday night, and as soon as the parents were asleep, Dana and Ahn limboed under the crisscross barriers into the secret chamber. They wore mittens and socks, so they'd leave no fingerprints or footprints. Dana carried a penlight that cast a circle of light no bigger than a Ping-Pong ball.

The plug of light matched Ahn's crawling along the walls, under the cots, looking for anything the police might have missed. Ahn flipped the thin straw mattresses, sending up a cloud of dust that made her sneeze.

"Sneeze quietly!" Dana hissed. "I wonder what this pottery thing is for."

"Chamber pot," Ahn said simply. "In my country everyone keeps one by the bed in case you have to *go* in the middle of the night."

"But it's empty."

"It's had 135 years to dry up."

"Gross."

They looked for buttons that might have popped off a shirt, or a hairpin, an earring: Nothing but dust and crumbs of decayed fabric.

"This is very discouraging," Ahn said, twisting her long black hair into a rope. "There isn't a single clue."

"I know." Dana sat in the center of the room, leaning against the cot where Elvira had lain. The penlight darted around the room like a scared rat. Maybe there *were* rats in this room! "Nancy Drew would have turned up something."

"Who's that? Did she go to your elementary school?" asked Ahn.

"Oh, I forget that you haven't been here forever. Nancy's a hotshot teenage detective. I've read about eighty Nancy Drew mysteries."

"Oh yes, while I was sailing across the world," Ahn said, as though the whole horrid experience had been a merry adventure. Actually, she had been the only one left to bury her parents in their village outside Saigon. Then she had come across the water in the bottom of a boat that wasn't very seaworthy, to join her two brothers and two sisters. In fact, it was very much the way the Africans had come to the New World in the 1600s and 1800s, only Ahn came by choice. "I guess we're no Nancy Drews," Ahn said.

"Shh, you hear something?" Dana turned out the penlight and put her ear to the wall. Footsteps! They each slid under a cot, breathing years of dust and mold and splintered wood. The parlor door opened, and there was a huge shadow in the backlight of the hall.

"Is anybody in there?" asked Dana's father.

She was tempted to whimper, "No."

Then her mother slipped into the room, in a flowing red kimono. "Jeffrey, don't tell me the girls are in here with the roosters."

"I'm sure they're not," Dana's father said, then he pronounced each word in a precise, menacing way, "because they know it would be against the law."

"And the police would nab them and ship them off to Leavenworth," her mother said, picking up on the game. "And next thing you know, they'd be starring in the sequel to *Women in Chains*."

"Well, let's close the door and go back to sleep," Dr. Shannon said, and the girls heard a loud banging of the door and exaggerated tramping around in the hall, then another door slamming.

"Don't be fooled, they're still out there," Dana whispered.

"I'm used to waiting in the dark," Ahn replied. They barely breathed, in that absolute blackness of the room where Elvira had died. Time passed—at least twenty endless minutes. There wasn't a sound in the hall.

"I think it's safe now," Dana whispered. "Let's sneak back to my room." They slowly slid out from under the cots and shimmied under the plastic barricade. Tiptoed across the wine-spill carpet. Dana turned the doorknob ever so slowly—not a squeak. The hall was black as the Wakarusa River. Suddenly Ahn stumbled over something. A body! She gasped: "Dana!" Then Dana put her foot on something soft and squishy and pulled it back. She flipped on the penlight. Two bodies lay sprawled across the floor—her mom in the red kimono, and her dad in his Mickey Mouse boxers.

"Wha? Wha's?" Her father bolted up and groped for the lamp switch nearby. "Wha's going on?"

"It's *The Escape of the Women in Chains*," Dana said. And she and Ahn scurried into her room and locked the door. They heard Dana's mother mutter, "We might as well go to bed, Jeffrey. We've been bamboozled."

Later, when they were through giggling and were debating about chancing it down to the kitchen for some Doritos and bean dip, Ahn turned serious. "I really wish we'd been able to find a clue in there."

"Ahn?"

"Hmm?"

Dana felt around under her bed for the little black journal. "Look what I have."

Ahn caught her breath as she read the title page. "You found this in *there*?"

"Last week."

"Who's Millicent Weaver?"

"The lady who owned this house, I think, when Elvira was here."

"The murderer?" Ahn asked, her eyes wide.

"I don't think so. She helped slaves escape. Listen to this."

"May 7, 1856—A man came to the door in the middle of the night. It's a wonder I heard him. He was bent and old, I thought maybe 70, but these Negroes age fast what with the lives they have. He'd been walking for six nights and was half delirious, afraid to ask directions. He saw my flag and thought he knew what it meant, but by the time he'd found our door, he no longer cared if he'd be captured and sent back. I made a pallet for him on the floor in front of the dying embers of the fire. He hadn't the energy to eat. I broke bread into little pieces and placed them on his tongue, as the Catholics do Communion wafers. I held his head so he could drink some warm camomile tea. And that's when I saw the strange markings on his ears. They'd notched him like a hog, dear Lord, so his master could always claim him."

"Oh Dana," Ahn cried. "Such a thing, even in this country?"

You Ain't Seen Nothin' Yet!

May 20, 1856

They had school only three months of the year, but somehow they accomplished as much as James had covered in a whole year in Boston. Miss Malone was working them like beasts of the field.

James had all of his books and a pen and ruler and his sketchbook in a canvas bag slung over his back. No telling where Jeremy Macon and Will Bowers had tossed their books. He walked between them, and they were boxing at his shoulders and ears in a playful way. "Just kidding, can't you take a joke?" they said, but James thought they were doing their best to provoke him into punching back. Well, in a minute—

They passed Bethany Maxwell's house, and Jeremy jerked his shirt down so he'd look less like a rabble-rouser in case Bethany happened to be peeking out from behind those prissy blue lace curtains. James barely lifted his head, so Jeremy wouldn't see him watching for Bethany, but he thought he saw her walk past an upstairs window, and his heart leaped.

"Will you look at that," Jeremy said, pointing to Mount Oread. A mere bump on the face of the earth, it nevertheless towered over the city of Lawrence, and now it seemed to be crawling with men.

James took advantage of the diversion to slip away from his friends. Friends, hah! Not like the boys back home, but better than no one.

Will said, "What do you think they're doing up there? Ain't no picnic."

"Looks like they're fixin' to go to war," Jeremy said, and he and Will gleefully rubbed their hands together as if they were warming them over a potbellied stove.

James studied the hill. There were not just men up there, but horses and tents. Looked like they'd be camping there for a good long time. Smoke swirled up from a campfire as if it'd been called out by a snake charmer.

"Want to climb up and investigate?" Will asked.

"Not on your life, moron," Jeremy answered. "Those men look mean and evil as weevils."

Mean? How could Jeremy tell from so far away? And evil, well, that was something altogether different. But just the same, James thought they should head home. "Well, my pa's expecting me to help him butcher a hog," he said, though it wasn't true, and his father wouldn't have the first inkling about which end to butcher, and which end to kiss.

"We butcher hogs in the wintertime, city boy."

Just then they noticed a few horses trailing down the mountain. Three, four? The horses got closer, and James's heart began to synchronize with the cloppity sound of their hooves. Looked like trouble.

But it was just three men on not very spectacular horses—a patchy-looking bay and two dapples that sure weren't thoroughbreds. The lead rider nosed up to James.

"I'm Deputy U.S. Marshal William Fain, here on Federal business." James stepped aside to let the horses pass. "These boys is my posse." The posse looked newly deputized and not too fearsome. James's heart slowed down.

Will asked, "What you in town for, Marshal Fain?"

"Looking for slave stealers."

"You ain't gonna find none here," Jeremy said. "We're every one of us law-abiding citizens. James Weaver's pa, he's even a lawyer."

But Marshal Fain wasn't about to be put off by a mangy flock of boys. "There's people been stealing the Nigras, and there's people been hiding 'em out."

James's chest tightened. Should he run for home? But what if the marshal got suspicious and followed him home and went after Ma? What if he asked had they seen any runaway slaves, and Rebecca blabbed it all out about the ones that had been sleeping in their bedrooms and attic, sometimes so many of them that they put bedrolls all over the floor and had to eat in shifts. Too risky. So James stayed put.

People came out of the Round Corner Drug Store to see what was going on. Mr. Bonds, who had a seed store, left it unattended, and some mourners streamed out of the funeral parlor, and a ladies' sewing circle broke up from the Unitarian Church, and suddenly the streets were swarming with Lawrence folks.

James saw Mrs. Bonds sidle up to her husband. A big elephant of a woman, she held a rifle flat against her flank.

Marshal Fain slid off his horse and shouted for everyone to be quiet. He showed his badge around in a wide circle. The sun caught it just so, and James winced. Everyone got quiet. Marshal Fain parked himself in the doorway of the Free-State Hotel, and he made a little speech that no one much admired.

"We aim to clear Nigra stealers out of this town, authority of the government of the *U*-nited States of America."

The Lawrence people booed and yelled. "Run him out of town!" one cried. "Out of the country!" another said. "Kansas Territory is free soil!"

One woman elbowed her way through the throng and spit at the marshal.

He wiped the spit off with the back of his hand and yelled, "Once a slave, always a slave, even on so-called free soil. I want every one of them Nigras back, and every slave stealer behind bars."

"Go jump in the Wakarusa!" Mrs. Bonds yelled, while her husband tried to shush her.

A member of the posse motioned to the marshal for attention. "I'm General Atchison," he bellowed, upstaging the marshal. His voice boomed above the din of the crowd: "My mama taught me every lady was to be respected. But if she's carryin' a Sharps rifle, she's no longer worthy of respect. I say, by God, trample her under your feet as you would a snake!"

Then Mr. Bonds picked up a sizable stone and hurled it at the general. All hell broke loose. The men swarmed Marshal Fain and the posse. Mrs. Bonds fired her rifle into the air. Will and Jeremy couldn't wait to get into the fracas, and they pushed forward with their fists swinging. Marshal Fain grabbed them both with his beefy arms.

"Get your hands off those boys!" cried Mrs. Bonds. "Somebody, run get their daddies."

That's what James could have done to help, but he was locked in place, sure as if his feet were nailed to the ground. Anyway, Will and Jeremy broke loose, just as a troop of men rushed toward the marshal again, their arms raised viciously.

"Hold it, hold it," yelled the editor of one of the Lawrence papers. "He's a Federal official."

"Better believe it," the general muttered.

"Look out!" someone yelled. Jeremy and Will backed off toward James. In a minute, quick as a calf is roped, Mr. Bonds was handcuffed behind his back, and so was his missus. The marshal grabbed up her rifle before a Lawrence man could scramble for it.

Then a larger posse rode down from Mount Oread, some dozen men with muskets and bayonets. Each led a barebacked horse. Suddenly it seemed like half the men in town were under arrest, though Lord knew where the marshal would keep all the prisoners, because the Lawrence jail only held three drunks, at best.

Somehow Marshal Fain got their attention again and

shouted, "I'm confident we've got all the trouble-causers and Nigra stealers, and if you'll just clear a path for us, we'll be on our way to Lecompton."

The posse loaded the prisoners onto the horses—not necessarily one to a horse, and they rode off. A fierce-looking tiger of a man, a Missouri Border Ruffian for sure, was bringing up the rear. He turned back to the women and children, frozen like trees in the street, and he roared, "You ain't seen nothin' yet!" Then, instead of following the marshal's parade to Lecompton, he yanked his horse around and galloped back up to the men watching from Mount Oread.

It was turning dusk. James picked up his book bag and felt a wrenching certainty, like something being tugged out of his gut: Come morning, those men would be down here.

But not in threes and fours. In the hundreds.

CHAPTER NINE

Edmund Wolcott's Castle

"Caleb Weaver, he's the man who built the house, or had it built." Dana's father read from a library Xerox copy. "Built it in 1856, which is when the Massachusetts Emigrant Aid Company sent his family to homestead out here."

Dana's mother was driving their rattly 1978 Honda, on their way to the Thoreau Middle School Spring Musicale, the last blast of the school year before they were sprung for the summer.

Dana asked, "And what about Mrs. Weaver?"

Her father scanned the paper. "Nothing on her. Mister was a lawyer, though."

Dana's mother said, "Missus was—what else?—a wife, a mother, a cook, and a maid. Things were pretty set in their day. Women weren't blessed with two full-time jobs like we are now." She was a speech clinician at the Kansas

School for the Deaf, and she could sign as well as she spoke. Now she flashed a few heated signs at a driver who was turning left without a signal.

"I'm glad I don't have to translate *that* to the listening audience. Val, you're crawling up his back!"

"He's a creep, and a terrible road hog."

"Dad, do you know if the little room was in the original house plans?"

"Can't tell, but I doubt it. It sounds like the house was a lot smaller. It had just two bedrooms upstairs, or one bedroom and a loft, and another bedroom downstairs. No third floor, no rooms in the attic like we have now. And, no indoor plumbing."

"Of course not," Dana's mother said. "Mrs. Weaver hauled raw sewage outside in buckets every day. Gave her a hard body. Women didn't need to work out at health clubs back then."

Dana's dad laughed and jiggled a bit of his wife's extra padding. "They were solid religious types, too, I'll bet."

"Quakers."

"Does it say that in the diary?" Dana's father was dying to see it, but the time still wasn't right.

"I haven't gotten through the whole thing yet, because the writing's really hard to read. It's small and close together, like Mrs. Weaver only had one little notebook, and she had to make it last."

"Oh look, Jeffrey, that's the Edmund Wolcott house you were telling me about. I can't believe they're going to tear it down."

Dana ducked to get a better look. The house was a limestone castle, looming three stories above the jungle of a yard. A lot of the windows were broken, and whole chunks of the limestone were eaten away by wind and rain. From the back, a tower jutted up, like the kind Rapunzel would have flopped her golden hair down from. Each of the upstairs bedrooms had a balcony, big enough for two persons only, with tattered awnings sheltering it.

"Check out the front door," Dana's father told them. It was two levels high, triple-wide, and knobby with intricate carvings. "This guy was loaded. A cattle baron, I read."

Dana said, "I'm surprised you didn't make us buy this monstrosity and turn it into a bed-and-breakfast."

"I really hate to see it torn down—"

"Don't get any ideas, Jeffrey." Mrs. Shannon gunned the engine as the light changed to green.

"Was this house around in Elvira's time?"

"Who?" her mother asked.

"Our dead body. Ahn and I call her Elvira."

"Doubtful," her father replied. "It looks like 1870s vintage to me, not 1850s. And besides, Edmund Wolcott didn't move here with the first wave of settlers."

"So he never hid slaves?"

"Or owned them."

"Dad, do you think our house was a station on the Underground Railroad?"

Her father wriggled his grayish beard and settled into his History Professor mode—eyes a hundred years away, finger stroking his forehead. "Well, it's unlikely. Both the known stations in the Lawrence area were outside the city. There was one over near Lone Star, just southwest of here, and some Major Abbott person ran a hot stop about five miles south of what used to be the southern edge of Lawrence. Most of the activity was in Topeka and Leavenworth, though."

"But suppose Elvira came to the house on her way north. Say she ran away from a plantation."

"More likely she was the Weavers' servant."

Dana shook her head. "Not a chance."

"Well, what makes you so sure, Miss Expert on Pre–Civil War Conditions?" her mother asked. "Oops!" She just missed clipping a station wagon, on her way into a tight-shoe parking place a good half mile away from Thoreau.

"Why do I ever let her drive?"

"Because you have two speeding tickets?" Dana's mom sweetly replied.

Dana said, "I'm just sure Millicent Weaver wouldn't have a black servant. I think she got sealed into the room."

"Dana, that's horrible!" cried her mother.

"Go with the theory. Why?"

"I don't know yet. See what you can find out at the library, Dad, and I'll sort of do my own research."

She watched her parents exchange glances. It was the 'she's-following-in-your-footsteps, Jeffrey' look, oozing into the 'haven't-we-done-a-fine-job-of-parenting!' look.

Her mom and dad communicated so well, with a click of the tongue, a shorthand language undecodable to outsiders, a simple tap of the finger that signaled annoyance, a burst of laughter when everyone else was wallowing in misery. This was how marriage was supposed to be, wasn't it?

So how on earth did Millicent Weaver keep such a big secret from her husband?

Later that night Dana turned to a page in the journal that troubled her so much every time she read it that she'd not been able to read past it yet.

May 14, 1856—Caleb's representing Barnaby Watts, who's been charged with helping a Negro escape. But Thou knowest full well what Mr. Weaver's saying outside the courtroom.

"The man's in flagrant disregard for the law, Millicent. The law's clear: The slave owner has every right to get up a posse, ride into free territory, and if he can prove it's his slave, take him right back to the South. Every right."

"Deuteronomy, Caleb. 'Thou shalt not deliver unto his master the servant which is escaped from his master to thee.'"

"Yes, yes."

"And Isaiah 16:3. 'Hide the outcast; betray not him that wandereth.'"

"Yes, yes."

His eyes filled with such agony that I wanted to pull him to me. But I didn't. Oh Lord, I didn't. I despised the sound of my own voice. I said, "Well then, Mr. Weaver, how can thee possibly represent Barnaby Watts in the courtroom?"

"Millicent, thee knows I'm torn. On one side there's God's law, and on the other side, man's law."

"And thee's pulled on thy reins and backed away

from God's law." As soon as the words were out, my face was hot with fury.

For fourteen years this man and I have shared bed and board, and how little we know one another this night.

A tear dropped to the page, and Dana quickly flicked it away so it wouldn't soak into the ancient, thirsty paper. She wondered what it was like for the children, for James and Rebecca, to have to keep such a secret from their father, to live in the stiffling atmosphere of the strain between their parents.

Maybe it was quickly resolved. Maybe in the next page. She made herself turn the page and flattened it to the left. The handwriting seemed different, as if a good many days or weeks had passed since Millicent Weaver had made an entry in the journal. Dana took a deep breath and read the cramped script.

But then the afternoon of May 21, the fire swept through the house and blew all our personal agonies aside. . . .

CHAPTER TEN

Thirty Cannonballs

May 21, 1856

There came a ferocious banging on the door, and it wasn't even dawn yet. James jumped out of bed and yanked his britches on. He was down the ladder to the front door before his parents were out of their bedroom.

Jeremy, with his hair all wild, yelled, "James, something's brewing out here."

"What's happening?" He thought of the men massing restlessly on Mount Oread last night. What were they up to?

"They're fixin' to come down from the mountain, hundreds of 'em, maybe thousands. My pa's organizing the men. We ain't letting 'em ride over us, you can bet on that."

"Son?" James's father came to the door, Ma right behind him, rolling her blond crimped hair into a knot.

"Morning, Mr. Weaver, ma'am. My pa says to get all the women and children out to the ravine at the edge of town, and all able-bodied men's to come to the Free-State Hotel. Armed."

Pa ignored Jeremy and turned to James. "Tell us what thee knows, son."

"There were these men up on the mountain, Pa, the marshal's posse I told you about, took the prisoners yesterday? The marshal left, but the men camped there all night."

"More of 'em than yesterday. Hundreds of 'em, sir. Proslavers, Border Ruffians from Missouri."

"But have they caused any trouble?" Pa asked.

"Well sir, they've taken over Governor Robinson's house for their headquarters. We ain't waitin' to be trampled by their horses, sir, all due respect." Jeremy tipped his cap toward Pa, but it seemed like an empty gesture.

"Have they made any threats, Jeremy?"

"Well sir, in the night they rolled this cannon into town. Old Sacramento, it's called, sir. Pa says it's left over from the war with Mexico. They brought it up from Georgia."

Pa thought about that a minute, while Ma went to start the stove warming.

Jeremy shifted from foot to foot, impatient with Pa's silence. "Sir, Old Sacramento's fixed square at the mouth of the Free-State Hotel. They aim to blow it to pieces. You might call that a threat. Sir."

Pa nodded. "Thank you, son. Thee must go on to the next house, as thy father told thee to, and we'll do what we have to."

With Jeremy gone, Ma began packing a basket of food. "James, wake thy sister and tell her to come down with a warm shawl and her favorite plaything, and not to dawdle a minute."

"Yes, Ma."

Pa said, "I'll wake thy sister, James. Thee must go out back and dig a hole. We'll bury whatever's dearest to us. But be quick, son."

The hole was easy; the ground was soft with spring rain, and when he was done he came in to find Rebecca, dwarfed in Pa's rocker, rubbing her eyes and clutching her baby doll. Ma put a small crate in the middle of the room, and they each dropped in a few objects—some books and notebooks, a pen and a jar of ink, Ma's ruby brooch from Great-grandma Baylor, Pa's law certificate, Rebecca's yellow hair ribbons and a red bucket and shovel she prized. James took far too long deciding what to save, and finally he tossed in entirely unimportant things—a rabbit's tail and a puny sketch he'd made of their house in Boston.

Suddenly they heard a clap of thunder, but it wasn't gone in seconds as it should have been.

"Thundering horses," Pa said. "Millicent, thee and Rebecca take the food and go on over and find the other women gathering in the ravine." Ma nodded, and tied her bonnet under her chin. She crooked her finger, which was a sure sign that Rebecca wasn't to delay a single instant.

"James, come outside. Thee and I will bury this box." They lowered the box, as small as a baby's coffin, and tamped the fresh earth over it. "Now we'll head into town and see how we can be helpful to our neighbors."

In town, people were shouting bulletins at one another and running everywhere, but Pa walked at his dignified, steady clip, his boots pulverizing clods of dirt in the road. James had to take deep breaths to keep going so slow when everyone was passing them by. After a time he looked back on their house, which seemed so singularly deserted out there. In a whirlwind of prairie vengeance, it could be so easily uprooted.

But there was no time for such thoughts, because now they were in the heart of town, and coming up behind a human chain of strangers outside the Free-State Hotel. Their line was broken only by the cannon in the middle of the square. The men's heels dug into the dirt, their shoulders set, their necks stiff—ready warriors, against a handful of Lawrence men just digging the sting of sleep from their eyes. Some of their men with fighting spirits had spent their fight the day before. Now they slept in the Lecompton jailhouse. Who was left? Old men, young men of peace, and a few scrappy boys.

Sheriff Samuel Jones broke out of the battalion of men. He was the sheriff of Douglas County, but really a resident of Missouri. For a second James thought the sheriff would be doing his duty as a law officer, but he soon made his mission clear. He climbed up on a barrel and cast his booming voice into the crowd. "Listen, men of Lawrence, we're through talking. My men's giving you thirty minutes to get everybody out of the hotel, and then, I swear to God, we'll fire on it."

No one stopped to question his word. People scurried every which way, pouring out of every door of the hotel with suitcases and boxes. Women tossed tables and mirrors, even small children, out the window, into the arms of the men below, while the marshal's posse swarmed into the hotel and ransacked the place. At the front door they manned a wagon where they loaded all the things they'd pilfered from the hotel—clothes and cans of food, sacks of potatoes, bedspreads, and anything they could lift in a dash.

Outside, children ran; women unaccustomed to running ran as fast as their cumbersome dresses would allow to the outskirts of the city, on the shouted orders of their fathers and husbands. Bethany Maxwell ran by, never even noticing James.

He stayed close to his father, waiting for a signal. What was a twelve-year-old expected to do? He wasn't a baby to cower with the women and children in the ravine, but he wasn't a man, either.

The posse raised their red flag over the Free-State Hotel.

"Smoke!" someone yelled. Behind them black ropes billowed toward the turquoise sky of the dawn. They captured puffs from the cottonwood trees in their wake. Then a giant flame stabbed the sky and turned it bright orange, as if the day had burst.

Sheriff Jones shouted, "I am determined to execute the law if it costs me my life!" and he gave the signal to fire the cannon at the hotel. A woman leaped from a third-floor window. James ran forward to soften her fall. He rolled to the ground and tasted dirt, then quickly helped the lady to her feet. Her thank-you was a scared smile as she ran off. Another cannonball. But the proud, stubborn walls of the hotel that harbored the free-state forces refused to crumble—even after thirty cannonballs were volleyed.

The proslavers, maddened by their failure, roared like

taunted lions. They rushed toward the hotel with powder kegs. Jeremy and Will and their fathers and a handful of other men tried to stop them, but the Lawrence men were shoved aside by the vicious mob. Two kegs of powder made their way down to the basement of the hotel. That's all it took. A spark of fire did what thirty cannonballs couldn't. The Free-State Hotel exploded and burned to the ground.

Sheriff Jones yelled, "I have done it, by God, I have done it! This is the happiest day of my life."

Now the Border Ruffians were pumped with their glory. Shouting, "Slavery in Kansas, slavery in Kansas," they rampaged through Lawrence. Burned both newspaper offices, but not before they took all the type out and threw it in the river. Robbed and terrorized the people in the streets and the few old folks who huddled in their homes.

Where were the Beecher's Bibles now? James shouted to Jeremy, "Where are those Sharps rifles?"

"Couldn't get any more ammo," he shouted back. He'd covered his face with a kerchief, because the smoke was as thick as clouds. "Don't breathe it, James!"

James pulled his collar over his nose and mouth. All around him, men were gasping for breath, coughing; black spit shot from their mouths. He lost Pa. Where was Jeremy? He spotted him now, throwing punches at one of the proslavers. And Will, who was bigger than all the boys their age, had wrestled another proslaver to the ground and was pummeling his face with the mallet of his fist.

Blood flew everywhere, turned the rich earth to mud.

A shot rang out, another and another. A piece of someone's hand flew by James's face. Proslavery, antislavery? He only knew he was splattered with its blood. His stomach heaved at the rusty, visceral stench.

Now he was scared. Scared he'd get hurt, and scared he'd run. Scared he'd bloody someone if he got in there like Will and Jeremy, and scared he'd kill someone, and scared he'd be glad he did it. He wanted to rush forward; his knees locked. Then he felt a tug at his arm. Pa.

"This is no place for men of God to be." His father yanked him so hard that he staggered and fell to the ground where he'd be trampled by the ugly mob. Pa pulled him back up, carried him like dead game, until they were in a clearing. He put James down, but pulled him close to his own chest.

"Thee must never harden thy heart to what thee's seen today."

James spoke through hot tears, his words thick and bitter as castor oil. "But we did nothing to help, Pa. They destroyed our whole town, and we watched."

"God requires us to be witnesses, son, not murderers. Come, we'll go home."

But there was no home, only the stones of the cellar, the broken skeleton of the second story, the heap of crumbled sod; burning earth stung their noses and throats. And all their worldly possessions lay smoldering.

Except for the few things they'd buried in the yard.

CHAPTER ELEVEN

The Sack of Lawrence

The movie was one of the Freddys, and it felt really good to scream and dig her nails into Mike Gruber's arm. Mike pumped popcorn into his mouth in steady rhythm. "It's not that scary," he said, with his eyes glued to the screen. In the flickery light, he looked green. Sally, Derek, everyone looked ghoulish. Only Ahn seemed unaffected. She watched the movie as if it were a video on photosynthesis.

Afterward, they all went to a frozen-yogurt shop where Dana's dad was to pick them up at eleven o'clock—but discreetly, invisibly.

"Cool movie," Derek said. "I liked Part Two better, though." Derek didn't bother ordering a sundae, just a long spoon so he could eat everybody else's.

They had a juicy argument over whether Part 2 or Part 3 was scarier, with gruesome evidence from each, as compared to Part 4 and Part 5. "The thing is, those were more violent, but less psychologically terrifying," Mike said.

"I'd have been happy to stop with the original," said Sally, swirling her white-chocolate sundae into mush.

"Nobody asked me, but I think the movies are stupid," Ahn told them. "Not like real."

Derek dared her: "Name one thing scarier you've ever seen."

"The bones in Dana's upstairs," she said quietly. "It's really scary to think what happened to that girl. Scarier to think we might not ever know. Tell them about the fire, Dana."

"My house burned down."

"What!" Mike yelled, and a gray-haired pair of dumplings across the room gave him a searing look.

"Well, it was 135 years ago."

"Oh, I see, it spontaneously regenerated. Did you know you can chop off a piece of a flatworm anywhere, and it'll grow itself back?"

"Very interesting, Mike."

"Gross," Sally wailed.

"Hey, I just presented the example to explain how Dana's house grew back."

"Drop it, Gruber," Derek said. "Tell us what happened with the fire."

"My house was sacked. Remember last year on Kansas Day Paul Cardenas did that oral report on the Sack of Lawrence?"

"I don't remember. I must have been home in the *sack* that day," Mike quipped.

"Or *sacked* out in the back of the room."

"Not bad, Derek. Or ran-*sacking* someone's locker."

"I don't get it," Ahn said.

"Subtleties of the language, kid. Idioms," said Mike.

"Idiot," Derek muttered.

"Dana, what are they talking about?"

"Well, Ahn, it's hard to explain, guys being so immature and all."

Mike sat up straight as a piccolo and said, "Tell us about the Sack of Lawrence, oh, please, please?"

"Not because you asked." Dana deliberately turned her back on Mike. "They practically burned the whole town down in 1856."

Sally asked, "Even the university?"

"This was before it was built," explained Dana. "And here's the weird part. Lawrence wasn't burned just once. Twice. After the first time, they rebuilt everything superfast because everyone was so mad and so determined to outsmart those proslavery guys. Then, seven years later some crazy named Quantrill bops into town in a Confederate uniform with a few other lunatics, and they go on this orgy of murder and mayhem. Oh, but they're chivalrous knights. They spare all the women and children. Shoot about 140 men, though, and burn down a couple of hundred businesses and homes. Nice guys."

Mike asked, "Your house got hit a second time?"

"I don't think so."

"How do you know?" asked Sally.

"Tell them how we know, Ahn."

Ahn's elfin face clouded over with sadness. "Because Elvira was already dead. She was already sealed in that room."

*   *   *

Dana's father dropped everybody off, and at the last minute Ahn invited Dana to spend the night at her house, *if* she brought the journal. Staying at Ahn's was always an adventure. Where Dana's house had eleven rooms, twelve counting Elvira's tomb, Ahn's had three rooms. There was one for the brothers, one for the sisters, and one for cooking, eating, and watching TV. But because all the brothers and sisters were older than Ahn, and went to high school or college and also worked at all the 7-Elevens in town, there was never a time when everyone was home. Also, there was never a time when no one was home. So Ahn and Dana got into their giant sleeping Ts and piled their pillows in a corner of the sisters' room, to read some more of the journal. Since the fire, they'd promised they'd only read it together. Ahn found the page quickly.

"May 31, 1856—There is good in all Thy works. With our house destroyed, I have left this slave-escape enterprise behind me. James and Rebecca are overjoyed. We have taken refuge with the Macons. Their house miraculously escaped the ravages of flame. It's quite crowded, all of us together, but the Macons are fine Christian folk and we are all making do. Caleb's gone to Topeka for a few days. When he returns, we'll set about rebuilding.

"Some of the men had a wood sawyers' tournament, so there would be logs aplenty for all the building. Young Will Bowers's father won by a count of three logs. His back wall went up first, as his prize.

"We're fortunate that we've money to buy lumber from the mill. Thy kindness is ever-bountiful."

Ahn said, "Here Millicent just tells about how they rebuilt your house. All the neighbors helped. Very nice." She skimmed a few pages. "This entry is dated June 14, 1856."

"The United States Congress has refused to accept Caleb's constitution. Oh, Lord, all his work on the side of right. Caleb laments that we shall not become a state this year, and not without more bloodshed."

"June 18, 1856—I am weary to the bones, for we've moved into the first floor of our house today, the hottest day yet of the summer. There's still the upstairs to finish, and Mr. Madison and his apprentice are working at that. There are so many houses to build since that horrid day. James is too old to sleep in a loft. Mr. Madison's building him a proper room."

"How old do you think James was?" Ahn asked.
"Our age?"
"Maybe a little older."
"Maybe he was shaving already."
"How old is that? My brothers are in college and they don't shave much."
"Asian men are different. I think James was extremely hairy."
"If you like them that way," Ahn said skeptically.

"Okay, go on."

Ahn skimmed the page. "This is just dull things about wood, the split logs for the floor, how they quarried the stone for the fireplace. Oh, look at this—"

"I've asked Mr. Madison to build a good-sized closet in the north bedroom. It would be a place where James could play his violin without making us all grind our teeth. Thou knowest, Lord, that James is a sincere musician, but not a gifted one."

"He played the violin? How romantic!" Dana cried.

Ahn read on. "June 20, nothing much. June 22, oh, this is sweet."

"I do believe these are the happiest days Caleb and I have shared. What with the constitution business temporarily put aside, we've been like a bride and groom feathering our new nest. I blush to write, he's been courting me! James watches out the corner of his eye. I believe he's of an age."

"At least puberty," Dana said. "At least we're in the right ballpark." But Ahn was deeply engrossed in the journal and didn't answer.

"Dana? Listen—"

". . . but then tonight, it all changed back. Caleb is in Leavenworth for the accursed trial of Barnaby Watts. The flag's no longer out there, but somehow the girl knew to come here, and now. She knocked on the door, good and firm, and I thought it was Edna Macon come for a cup of tea. But there stood this girl, small and sure in manner, speaking like a Southern lady. But she is as dark as the tree outside my window. She says Thou sent her to me. She says she will never get to Canada, but she's meant to help others on their journey. My stomach did somersaults when I saw how unwavering she was. Now I eagerly await—and dread—tomorrow's sunrise."

Ahn put the journal down thoughtfully, and when she lifted her eyes to Dana, they both said, "Elvira's here."

CHAPTER TWELVE

Follow the Drinking Gourd

June 1856

So, it's starting up again, James thought. Pa was off defending the man they said was a slave stealer, Ma was hiding runaways, and he and Rebecca were expected to keep their mouths shut. The unfairness of it all hit him like the snap of a wet sheet when he came down from his new room and found the girl peeling potatoes, as if she'd always been there. Ma stoked the coal stove and greeted him without turning around.

"Welcome to a new summer day. James, shake hands with Miss Lizbet Charles."

James wiped the morning sweat off his hand and stuck it out. The girl, Lizbet, wiped potato starch down her apron and shook his hand. "Morning, Mr. James Weaver. You don't look a bit like your sister." She looked him right in the eye, not like the others who'd come to the house.

Something was wrong here. Miz Lizbet was no ordinary runaway slave. As soon as he saw his ma's face—working her lips like dough, eyelids shading frightened eyes—he wondered what hold this young Negro had over his mother. And at the same time, he just knew Ma had given her leave to stay with them: She wouldn't be moving on by nightfall, like the others.

Miz Lizbet must have understood some of the dread in his face. "Your family's kind to let me stay a spell," she said haughtily, as if she had it coming. There wasn't a hint of a smile in her voice, and her speech was so schoolteacherlike, not like the other runaways who'd picked up words hurdy-gurdy.

Ma couldn't get the stove lit. "Well, it's too hot to cook anyway," she said. "We've got some cold meat pie from last night, and peaches, and a bit of bread pudding I put by. We'll make do."

"Ma, I'm going down to the river with Jeremy and them. Too hot to do much but swim and fish on a day like this."

"Yes, bring us home a fat catfish or two for supper. We'll cook the fish outside on an open fire."

That brought the first smile to Miz Lizbet. "Oh, I do love fried fish with that smoky fire taste."

"Fine," Ma said nervously. "Lizbet, would thee go down to the cellar and fetch the meat pie and a handful of peaches, please?" They'd built steps to the cellar *inside* the house—a modern innovation—and Ma pointed the way. When Miz Lizbet was out of earshot, Ma whispered,

"I'm called to this, James. She's asked me to teach her to read and write."

"Ma! Thee knows it's illegal to teach slaves to read."

"Lizbet is not a slave. She's a free Negro on free soil."

"It's starting up again, Ma, Rebecca and me wondering who we're going to find warming their feet by our fire." Ma had beads of sweat on her upper lip; it would be months before anyone would need to warm his feet. Why had he used that ridiculous example? But now he hit her with the big one: "And us lying to Pa."

Ma's nose flared, which was a sure sign she was trying to get herself easy again, so she wouldn't say something she'd be sorry about. "Thee must understand, James, each of us must answer to the voice within."

"But we were just getting happy out here in Kansas. Just starting to feel like maybe it could be home." Building the house a second time had done it for James. He'd sketched every step of the progress. Only yesterday he'd ripped up his baby sketch of the Boston house. He'd thrown the paper pieces into the Wakarusa, watched them bloat up and sink.

"James Weaver, I have been waiting for a sign. Lizbet is the sign. Thee must learn to accept what God demands of us."

"Of thee, Ma, not of me."

Ma reached out and gently raked his hair across his brow. "I must take a pair of shears to thy hair, or thee won't be able to see thy supper."

He jerked away from her touch. "Jeremy and them, they go to a barber."

"And will thee be having some tailor sew thy clothes,

74

and will thee be taking thy meals at a boardinghouse?"
Ma asked crossly.

"Who's more important to thee—some slave girl, or
thy family?" There, it was out.

Ma locked her arms across her chest, and James knew
she was deep in prayer. Her chest rose and fell as if she
were sleeping, her nose flared. He tried to pray but only
felt the silence that echoed in the new wood-paneled
room. Finally, he heard Miz Lizbet's footsteps coming up
from the cellar.

"She stays," Ma whispered.

The catfish was crisp and salty, and the potatoes, too,
fried in a big pan over the campfire. A pile of fish heads
and bones lay on the ground, and Rebecca poked at the
eyes with a twig.

"Thee can pop them out for marbles," she said gleefully. The Kansas evening was steamy already. They had
no need for more heat, so Miz Lizbet doused the fire with
a slug of water from a bucket. While the fire sizzled,
James stole a look at her face, grayed by the dusk and the
slant of moonlight.

Ma caught him looking. "Lizbet tells glorious stories."

"Tell us one, tell us one!" Rebecca begged.

She didn't need much prompting. "There's a man
named Henry Brown," she began.

"Was he a white man?" Rebecca asked.

"He was a black man. Could have been my uncle. A
man who worked in a tobacco factory in Virginia. A slave
man. Amen." The cadence of her speech was so musical
that James was lured into the story. "A braver man you

can't imagine, a man who dreamed of making free. So deep and wide was his yearning for freedom, he did something that could have delivered him to lonely death."

"What did he do?" Rebecca whispered.

"Henry Brown of Virginia, he heard the voice of God, said, 'Go get a box and put yourself in it.' Had himself sealed in a box, box shaped like a coffin."

"Oh, he couldn't!"

"Could and did, Rebecca Weaver. A God-sent white man, a carpenter like the other one, made him a box, nailed it shut, put five hickory loops wound round to keep the box fixed. Mailed him to Philadelphia. Amen."

"How long did he stay in the mail?" Rebecca asked, and Ma said, "Hush, child."

"No, let her ask questions. It's only when folks stop asking questions, we're in muddy waters."

No? A Negro had out-and-out said *no* to a white woman? James watched her more closely, drawn deeper into the rolling river of her voice.

"Twenty-six hours he traveled in that box. Tossed upside down, he was, blood pumping into his head, from Virginia to Maryland."

James wondered about the details—food, water, and so forth.

"But what happened when he had to make water?"

"Rebecca Weaver!"

"Don't know," Miz Lizbet said with a smile. "You go up to Philadelphia sometime, ask to see a man called Henry Box Brown, little man, not much bigger than me, and you ask him, 'What did you do twenty-six hours in that box, when you had to make water?'"

"Oh, Miz Lizbet, I couldn't!"

"Then listen. When that box, it got to Philadelphia, three men were waiting for him. First man knocked on the box; he thought he heard a tapping, but couldn't be sure. Second man rapped on the box with a hammer, and there wasn't a sound from inside. The third man, his heart beating fast, he didn't wait for an answering rap. He took his bowie knife, and he cut the hickory loops that held the box fixed. Those men, they pried the lid up, long nails came squeaking up through the wood. Pulled away the straw and cotton wool padding that kept Henry Brown from breaking his bones when that box was tossed from the train to the riverboat. And what do you reckon they found?"

James guessed, "His hair'd turned white and he was crazy as a loon?"

"Naw. Those three men, they fell back when Henry Box Brown stepped out of that crate and he said to them, 'How do you do, gentlemen?' Spry as a young buck, drenched in sweat, though. True story. Amen."

James was fixing the details in his mind to tell Jeremy and Will, only he wouldn't be able to tell them where he got the story, and they'd never believe it.

Miz Lizbet said, "Black folks find all different ways of following the drinking gourd."

James had heard a song with those words. Some of the men were singing it at the warming for a family whose house had just been rebuilt. "Follow the drinking gourd." He'd thought it was a bawdy song.

"Not a drinking gourd for spirits, surely," Ma said, her voice girlish.

"No, ma'am. Look up, see the sky. See how those stars make a dipper."

They all had their faces toward the darkening sky. "I don't see it," Rebecca said.

"Thee must draw a line in thy mind from star to star, child, and see if it doesn't look like a big water dipper."

Miz Lizbet added, "Now look for the brightest star at the handle end, see?"

James saw it—the North Star. Last spring he'd been amazed to find it in the sky here, just as it had been in Boston.

"Mr. James Weaver sees it. It's the North Star. When my brothers and sisters leave their shackles behind, we follow the North Star. Keep seeing the star, you know you're heading north to freedom. And while we're still down there, only just dreaming about making free, we look up at that star like we're doing tonight, the water dipper, too, and we sing so our masters don't know about the dream that's burning in our hearts. Sing, 'steal away home to Jesus,' sing 'wade in the water children,' sing 'follow the drinking gourd.'" Miz Lizbet chuckled. "White masters think we haven't got a thought in our heads."

"Thee tells it right pretty," James said, gazing at the stars that came as tiny explosions in the blackening sky.

CHAPTER THIRTEEN

The Conductor

Swine Flu was, without a doubt, the best band in Kansas, and because the drummer knew somebody, who knew somebody, whose mother was the librarian at Thoreau, Swine Flu played at the dance on the last night of school.

Dana's mother chaperoned the dance, with way too many other parents, and afterward she drove everybody home.

"Air-conditioning!" Sally gasped.

Dana and Ahn and Sally and Jeep and Derek and Mike were a jumble of jeans in the back, on the seat, the floor, on laps, while Dana's mother had the whole wide front seat to herself.

"Wasn't the band cool?" Sally said.

"It's the first dance we didn't have a DJ. Live music is so—live," said Derek. "They were great."

"They didn't take any requests."

"Everything sounded the same."

"Too much pop. Not enough heavy metal."

"No punk."

"No seventies."

"No rap."

"I liked everything except the songs they wrote themselves."

"They sure were great."

"Yeah."

Jeep asked, "What did you think of Swine Flu, Mrs. Shannon?"

"Well, I've given this a lot of consideration. I think they're loud, vile, uncoordinated, derivative, obscene, greasy, no-talent young men."

"I guess they were worth every penny, then," Mike said.

Since someone had already done the unpardonable and spoken to the chauffeur, Derek continued the breach of etiquette. "So, how's the dead body in your upstairs room, Mrs. Shannon?"

"Still dead. But the issue's not." A van came out of nowhere, and she had to swerve to miss it. "Maybe I should keep my mind on the road?"

Sally whispered, "I forgot how your mother drives. I was really hoping I'd live until high school."

"Hey, can you believe it, we're officially eighth graders!" Jeep yelled.

"Next year we'll be freshmen!"

"That's a sexist term, Derek."

"Okay, okay, freshpersons."

There was a lot of cheering and rearranging of the tangle of legs. Then Dana said, "Guess what my dad turned up about Elvira."

"El-VYE-ruh, El-VYE-ruh," Mike sang, in a crummy imitation of the Oak Ridge Boys.

"Good thing you're only the warm-up act, Mike. Actually, Elvira's name was really Lizbet Charles. We think she was a conductor on the Underground Railroad."

Ahn explained, "The conductors were the ones who led slaves on the trip north to freedom."

Jeep asked, "That's what old Elvira did?"

"Well, we don't know that much about her. There was just one paragraph my dad found in some book published in 1870. But it looks like she made about eight or ten trips back into the South to rescue slaves."

"And here's the amazing part," Ahn said. "All those people she led north, we think they slept in Dana's house."

Jeep said, "It gives me the creeps, those people getting stung with whips and being sold like cattle and not getting to stay with their wives or kids. It's pretty incredible they made it as far as your place, Dana. That house could be like a national historical monument, if it's all true."

"Except for the fact that an extremely dead person turned up in that house," Mike said. "I think they take off points for that."

"Don't you wonder what happened to her, really and actually?" asked Sally. "I mean, don't you wonder how she ended up dead?"

"Let's find out," Jeep said, and at that moment Dana decided she'd show him Millicent Weaver's journal sometime when the others weren't around.

Three First Names

July 1856

"Not whilst my husband's home!"

"They come when they come," Miz Lizbet said. Both women sewed bolts of gray fabric, but James noticed that Ma's done-end folded into a thick pile at her feet while Miz Lizbet struggled with every stitch.

"Thee doesn't understand," Ma said. "Thee may not bring thy pilgrims when Mr. Weaver is in the house."

"They come when they come," Miz Lizbet said again. "They come like the tide which God Himself can't hold back."

"Lizbet Charles, thee is the most stubborn mule of a woman I have ever encountered."

James looked up from his sketchbook to see if Ma had some teasing in her face, but her brow was wrinkled and her lips pressed tightly together as if she were holding pins. James was close enough to hear her grind her teeth. "My husband comes home tomorrow. Thee may not stay here any longer."

"Too soon," Miz Lizbet said.

"Tomorrow."

Miz Lizbet put her sewing aside and walked over to the cold grate of the fireplace. It seemed to James that she was ticking things off in her mind, a great list with check marks beside each item. Finally, she said, "I won't bring them to the door if the flag isn't out. I'll keep going with them to the next station."

"But if thee is here whilst my husband is in the house, thee must stay in the small room upstairs. Thee must not show thy face."

And so, James guessed, they came to some womanly agreement, because Ma said nothing more about Miz Lizbet leaving for a while.

"I sew much faster when I talk," she said, settling back into the rocking chair. She held her needle in midair; it never found the fabric. "Mr. James Weaver, have you heard about Miz Ellen Craft? She escaped in a wondrous way."

"No, Miz Lizbet," he said, trying not to sound too rude. That little prairie church he had in his mind just wouldn't come into clear focus on the paper. Must have been because Miz Lizbet was talking on and on.

"From Georgia, she was a brave woman, a slave. Amen."

"Amen," James said, thinking that would be the end of it.

"Her father was a white man, her master to be sure.

Miz Ellen Craft was light enough to pass for white. And she had a great love in her life. William Craft, he was. They were as married as slaves could be. This wasn't yesterday, or day before. This was eighteen and forty-eight—long time ago."

"She escaped? How?" Why was Ma encouraging Miz Lizbet?!

"Nearly Christmas, before dawn, Ellen and William left their cabin, said good-bye to no one, not even her mother. They went to the railroad station to begin their journey."

"Thee means the Underground Railroad?"

"No, ma'am. I mean the legal, above the ground, on the tracks, riding in a train railroad station. And Ellen Craft rode in first class, too."

"How was she able to manage that?" Ma asked, her flying fingers pulling thread through the fabric.

"She passed as a rich Southern planter gentleman in a fine black suit and cloak, some high-heeled boots with a glassy shine, a gentleman's top hat. But a half-blind cat would notice right away that this gentleman had no proper beard. So William fixed a muffler around Ellen's face like a poultice, as if she was ailing something fierce from a toothache. And those pretty-girl eyes, they hid behind thick green frame glasses."

"Very imaginative," Ma said, "but the Bible frowns on women dressing in the raiment of men."

"Yes, Miz Weaver, and the Bible frowns on treating human beings like beasts of burden. Why, I heard a preacher once say even the beasts of the field had a Sabbath day of rest. Mr. James Weaver, are you listening?"

84

"Yes, Miz Lizbet," he groaned. Maybe that steeple was just too tall. He lopped off the point by hiding it in clouds. Better.

"And that's not all. William did Ellen Craft up as an invalid, so no one would know she couldn't read or write like a gentlemen should. Put her arm in a sling so she couldn't sign the register in all those fine hotels where she put her head down each night. She hobbled with a cane. He said she was deaf so she'd never have to talk."

"What a sight she must have been!" Ma said.

"And William, he went with her as her manservant." Miz Lizbet laughed, took up her sewing again. "First time it wasn't the other way around, wife being the servant to the husband."

James asked, "Are you married, Miz Lizbet?"

"Was." The subject was clearly closed, and no one said anything for the longest time, which gave James some hope. Then she started in again. "Four days they traveled from Georgia to South Carolina to North Carolina to Virginia to Washington to Baltimore, and finally to Philadelphia. How many boats and trains would you guess, Mr. James Weaver?"

He had no idea. "More than six?"

"Three boats and five trains. And mind, neither one of them could read a sign, a ticket, a word of any language. Didn't dare ask anyone, either. It's a miracle they found their way."

"I guess they followed the drinking gourd," James said, slamming his book shut. "So, what happened?"

"Before the popping eyes of those white men in Philadelphia, Miz Ellen Craft transformed herself from a sickly Southern gentleman into a beautiful, strong woman. A preacher married them proper, and they went to Boston to give lectures. Got to be pretty famous."

"Why yes," Ma said, "I do believe I remember hearing about them."

"Amen?" James said.

"Not quite. Some president, his name was Millard Fillmore, he sent 600 soldiers to Boston to capture Ellen and William Craft. Imagine, 600 soldiers after two free black souls."

Amazing. Miss Malone never told them about this. "And then what happened?"

"Sailed for England very fast. A fugitive is safe there, not like here."

James was surprised to hear Ma ask, "Has thee a child?"

"No child, Miz Weaver. I lost my Matthew Luke Charles before we were blessed with a child. That's assuming getting born into slavery's a blessing."

"Tell us about Matthew Luke," James said.

"*Mr. Charles,* to thee, son."

"He had three first names," Miz Lizbet said with a chuckle.

"How did he die?" asked James.

"Well!" Miz Lizbet said indignantly. "You think I'm going to tell you how he died before I say how he lived?"

"Then how did he live, Miz Lizbet?"

"Very, very well," she replied, puffing up with pride. "Rich for a while, signing papers, meeting with all manner of businessmen."

"Mr. Charles, then, he wasn't an African?" James asked.

"Of course he was an African!"

Ma said, "A free man, no doubt."

"No, Miz Weaver, not a free man. He was the son of a slave, and he was the son of a slave master. Ouch!" yelled Miz Lizbet. "This needle came right up and stuck me." She popped her finger into her mouth.

"And so?" Ma gently prodded.

"I'm sewing as fast as I can, what with my finger bleeding."

"I mean, tell us more about thy husband."

Miz Lizbet peered at them over the finger she was sucking. "Time's not right."

"But, Miz Lizbet," James protested.

"Amen and selah," she said, and her lips were sealed.

CHAPTER FIFTEEN

Uncle Mose

"Hey, Jeep, you coming?" two of his church friends asked. They looked at Dana curiously, as people hurried by from store to store in the mall.

"In a minute. Go on."

"Yeah. We'll meet you over in the arcade." It was the first Monday of summer vacation, and the kids had about thirty things planned for the day. They seemed annoyed that Jeep was sitting on this bench with some redheaded girl, reading a stupid black book.

Dana read over his shoulder, although she hated when people did that to her.

July 5, 1856—We heard Caleb's wagon and hastened Lizbet up the stairs. I gave her a basket of food, her primer and copybook, and a chamber pot. She avidly promised she'd stay hidden while Mr.

Weaver was in the house. Rebecca, bless her sweet young heart, thinks it's a jolly adventure, but James does not approve.

Jeep asked, "Who's James?"

"Her son. About our age."

. . . but James does not approve. He's grown sullen. I miss the boy he was only a season ago.

Lizbet enchants us with such wondrous tales. One slave, Bog by name, feigned a seizure on the auction block. He fooled the doctor who examined him and was taken to a jail cell while the slave sellers considered what to do about him. Lord, Thou opened a door for the man. Bog escaped and is now living free in Canada.

"All right! One brother made it."

"Read the next one, Jeep."

In Iowa Point, Kansas, a man called Uncle Mose stood before a greedy mob on the auction block. Men came up to feel his muscles, check his teeth, look him up and down, as if he were a common beast of burden. This man was sold for a meager $200. Such a paltry sum as the measure of a man.

"Jesus," Jeep said.

"I'm sorry. Do you want to stop reading?" But Jeep had turned the page.

Whilst on the auction block, Uncle Mose saw a pack of some twenty-five men riding horses down the ravine. He feared they meant to swarm him and kill him, but it proved that these men were Free-Soilers bent on breaking up the auction. They fell into a violent brawl with the slave buyers, and in the confusion of flying punches, one of the Free-Soilers shouted to Uncle Mose, "The moment your feet touched Kansas soil, you were a free man!" Then he directed Uncle Mose to climb on the back of a riderless horse, and Uncle Mose rode off to freedom.

Jeep's eyes were somewhere else now, maybe seeing Uncle Mose ride through the ravine, north and west by way of Oskaloosa, where he'd be easily passed north to Nebraska. Maybe he saw Uncle Mose with a wife and family living in a log cabin in Canada and working as a blacksmith or a lumberjack for real wages. Maybe he saw Uncle Mose as his own great-great-grandfather.

Dana left Jeep to his dreaming and read the next passage.

July 9, 1856—I'm collecting these stories here in my journal. One day soon I'll share them with Caleb, and he'll accept why I harbor and feed these people; why I disguise them in Quaker dresses and bonnets and veils and send them on their way; why I hide Lizbet from Caleb; why James is so sullen and quick to anger. Please Lord, assure me that one day Caleb will understand why I am sacrificing my own dear family as if they themselves were on the auction block.

Jeep was on his feet, his hands jammed into his jeans pockets. "What happened to Elvira?" he said sharply. "I guess her name's really Lizbet. You think she was murdered by this Caleb guy?"

Dana shook her head. "Other places in the journal, it shows how Caleb makes a big case of being nonviolent. It would be like Martin Luther King aiming a gun at a guy."

"Listen, I'm going over to find my friends."

"Okay. Call me when you want to read some more." But he made no move to go. So she asked, "Jeep, what would you have done if you'd been alive then?"

"How do I know? What a dumb question." He jogged in place, on the balls of his feet. Dana waited. "I don't think I'd have been any Martin Luther King, though, if you get my message."

CHAPTER SIXTEEN

They Never Looked Back

July 1856

Ma fixed a picnic. "There's a generous breeze today, for July. Let's have a family day out-of-doors." But James knew the real reason Ma was getting them out: Miz Lizbet had been holed up in that little room a day and a half, and it had no window for air or light. Once they were in the wagon, Miz Lizbet could come out, have a bath, grab armfuls of fresh air, and be gone again to Missouri to fetch another group of fugitives.

At Quail Feather Creek, Pa sprawled on a blanket, Rebecca joggling on his belly. Ma bustled around packing up the chicken bones and dirty plates and cups, shaking out crumbs, folding the tablecloth.

The sun rose to its highest overhead peak, so bright orange that James couldn't look too long.

"It's almost too hot to be out here," Pa said, so Ma fanned him with the hem of her skirt. "Watch thee doesn't show too much of thy bloomers," Pa teased.

"Honestly, Caleb! Thee's incorrigible."

James listened to them as he flopped onto his belly, with a slack line lazily hanging into the creek. Maybe something would bite—besides mosquitos—and maybe it wouldn't.

"Sit a minute, Millicent, thee's buzzing like a queen bee. Ouch! Rebecca, thee musn't bounce so hard. I'm not a feather bed or a stack of hay. Go jump on thy brother's back."

"Pa!"

"Stay where thee is, little kitten, but purr soft awhile."

Rebecca feigned a purr that sounded like the roar of a steamboat.

"Caleb," Ma said, and James feared something serious was coming to break the spell of the carefree afternoon. He glanced back and saw her take Pa's hand in her lap. "About the Negroes—" Pa put his finger on Ma's lips.

Ma wisely changed the subject. "I've brought along a peach shortcake to take to the Olneys. Maybe we should start out for their place."

Dr. Olney had just brought his family out from Boston, because all the warring and burning had left so many people injured. James couldn't remember meeting the Olneys in Boston. He would have remembered a bald elf like Dr. Olney, and his wife whose chins ruffled on her chest.

As soon as Ma turned over the peach shortcake—

would they offer some before the afternoon was out?—Rebecca asked, "Does thee have any little girls to play with?"

"Not as big as thee, or as pretty," Mrs. Olney said. "But we have a pink round baby girl. Come, I'll show her to you." Rebecca and the women went inside gleefully. Ma called from the porch, "James, does thee want to see Olneys' baby?"

"Maybe later, Ma." Now, if it had been a rattler, or a thirty-pound tomato, or a two-headed calf that Mrs. Olney was showing off, he'd have gone to have a look. But a baby wasn't worth trudging through the house for. James stayed outside with the men, who didn't seem to notice that he was there at all.

Thunder had been unhitched from the wagon and was being watered by a man whose skin glistened with sweat like the horse's hide. In fact, he and the horse were nearly the same golden brown color. "Thank thee for looking after the horse, Solomon," said Dr. Olney. "She could use a bit of cool water on her back, I suspect."

James drew a castle in the dirt while the men talked about the orchestra in Boston and about a senator named Stephen Douglas who was still stirring up a nest of vipers with his talk about that Kansas-Nebraska compromise. A pile of wood lay nearby, with an axe sticking out of its flesh. James longed to sling that axe and split the logs—anything for some action while the men's voices droned in talk, talk, talk.

Here came a man on horseback, and Thunder didn't like him a bit. She started dancing nervously, and slapping the ground with her shoe. The Negro man Solomon looked up, and all at once it seemed the still, sluggish afternoon had turned to raging waters.

The man dismounted and seemed as tall as his horse. On his head slouched a sweat-ringed hat with a toothless feather stuck in it, and a bowie knife showed out the top of his boot. His carbine was slung over the ribs of the scrawny horse. His voice dusty and dry, he asked, "You the slave Deacon Barclay, master's Edwin Barclay of Macon, Georgia?"

"No sir. I'm a free man. Got papers to prove it."

"Thee is on my property, friend." Dr. Olney stood right up to the man, though he was about half the tyrant's size.

"Does thee have a warrant for the arrest of this man?" Pa asked.

"I don't need no warrant." He took a paper out of his saddlebag and snapped it in Solomon's face. "This here gives me all the authority I need to take Deacon back to Georgia."

"Friend," Dr. Olney said, "this man is Solomon Jefferson, and he came with my family from Boston. He's been free since he was a boy."

"Paper says otherwise."

Pa pulled out his spectacles. "May I see it?"

"No sir, I ain't falling for no tricks like y'all tearing it up or tossing it in the horse's trough." His horse drank greedily from that trough now.

James looked at Solomon to gauge how much fight was in him. He followed Solomon's eyes to the axe in the woodpile. The handle faced Solomon . . . so close . . . so easy.

The slave trader said, "Got me something else in my saddlebag." He yanked it out of his bag. "Brand-new-forged Smith & Wesson." James lurched forward as the man put the gun to Pa's head.

"All I want's the nigger. I can get me $500 for him. The rest of you's not worth a bucket of spit."

"Stay clear, James," Pa said, his voice strung tight.

James stared at the gun aimed at Pa's face and saw Pa ease into prayer, imagined him saying, "Yea, though I walk through the valley of the shadow of death, I shall fear no evil, for Thou art with me. . . ." That's when he realized what he could do. He stepped between the slave catcher and Solomon just long enough to let Solomon snatch up that axe, then James jumped out of the way.

Solomon's mighty arm raised that axe into the air. It could have come down on the man's head, could have split him right in two like a thick log. But Solomon had lived among Quakers too long. "Dr. Olney," he cried out, "shall I let the axe fall?"

"No!" Dr. Olney and Pa shouted it together.

And Solomon the free man dropped the axe to the ground and was a slave once more.

Now Solomon's hands were tied in front of him, with a rope that was also wound around his neck. The slave catcher had a good hold on the end of the rope. James was embarrassed to look at Solomon; he thought he'd be as dispirited as Thunder was when they first broke her. But instead James read something else in the man's dark face: Triumph.

"Thee goes with God."

"I believe so, Dr. Olney. God bless."

Pa said, "I'll do everything I can to get thee out again. Thee has my word, friend."

The man yanked on the rope, and Solomon stumbled.

"Thee means for him to walk?" Dr. Olney asked.

The slave catcher's laugh was dry and coarse. "Only got the one horse. I ain't walking, and I sure ain't riding cheek to jowl with no nigger."

"Wait." Pa led Thunder back, and Dr. Olney fetched a saddle. The two of them gently lifted Solomon to the horse, so as not to pull the ropes too tight. Thunder was used to pulling a wagon and she looked surprised when the weight of the man fell upon her back, but she trotted on behind the other horse. Neither Thunder nor Solomon ever looked back.

CHAPTER SEVENTEEN

The View from Lizbet's Cot

Jeep wanted to sit in the room, feel it from the inside out. He told Dana and Ahn, "Last summer I was in Chicago, and we went to the Museum of Science and Industry. They got everything there, but what blew me away was walking my little brothers right through a heart. It was all blue and red and see-through. Sound effects, too. You could hear it pumping."

"Would I like that?" Ahn asked.

"I don't know, but what I'm saying is, I want to sit in Lizbet's room and feel it pumping." So he slid under the off-limits strips while Dana and Ahn crouched at the door of the little room, trying to make sense of Jeep's movements.

He knocked on the wall every few inches. Was he looking for a hollow board something was hidden behind? He backed onto Lizbet's cot and carefully lay on the straw, staring at the ceiling, arms folded under his head.

"What are you thinking?" Dana asked.

"Nothing. I'm lying here trying to guess what *she* was thinking. Hey, go downstairs and come in the front door. I want to see if I can hear that from up here."

Dana and Ahn ran downstairs and tried to come in as quietly as possible, crept up the stairs like cats, and burst into the parlor. "Well?"

"I didn't hear a thing," Jeep said gravely. "They could have come home and trapped her." He rolled off the cot and flipped the mattress, running his hand over every inch of it like a doctor feeling for lumps. He took apart the crudely made frame of the cot, which was just unfinished boards notched into the crotches of other rough boards. He put it all back together.

Ahn whispered, "What does he think he's going to find that the police didn't?"

"Where was the diary?" Jeep asked.

"Between her bed and the wall."

Jeep crawled under the other cot. His hollow voice echoed from underneath: "She wasn't any bigger than me?"

"But she'd already had her growth spurt," Dana teased. Jeep was always griping about being so short and was living for his fourteenth birthday when he was sure he'd sprout eight inches.

He slid out like a mechanic rolling out from under a Chevy, crouched on the worn split logs, and didn't say anything for the longest time. Then: "She died in this room."

Ahn asked, "How can you be sure?"

"I just know it."

"I've read the whole journal, and there are no more clues. It just stops all of a sudden," Dana explained.

Jeep asked, "What's the last thing that happened?"

"Mrs. Weaver gets called to Boston because her father's dying: One day she writes that she's going, and the next twenty pages are totally blank."

"That's it," Jeep cried. "I know what happened to Miz Lizbet Charles, but what I don't know is just how it happened. Not yet."

"Tell us!" Ahn begged.

But Jeep shook his head. "I've got to work it around a little more and spend some time in the library." On his feet now, he suddenly bolted past them to the door. "I have to get home to baby-sit my little brothers so my mom can go to work."

Downstairs in the kitchen, Dana poured a glass of milk for Ahn. She trailed a cookie through her own milk.

Ahn asked, "Do you think Jeep really knows something?"

"I don't think we'll ever know anything for sure about Lizbet Charles."

£ike a Real Son

July 1856

Pa was gone to Missouri with legal papers to try to get Solomon back, and so Miz Lizbet had free rein of the house. She made James nervous as a rat, and besides, Rebecca was down with some fever, and Ma doctored and fretted over her until James thought he'd jump right out of his skin if he didn't get out of the house.

Outside, under the noonday sun, he thought he felt blisters raising on his skin, like dough frying in hot oil. In Boston there was the harbor and the brooding shade of gray buildings. There, your skin didn't sizzle in the sun like it did here.

James heard something sliding through the tall grass. A rattler! His eyes darted around until he spotted the axe. Two giant leaps back, and he'd have it in his hand, and whop! There'd be two ends of that snake grabbing for each other.

But it wasn't a rattler. It was only a prairie wolf, small as a househound. The bloody carcass of a rabbit hung from its mouth, and it threw its head this way and that as it tore at the meat. Spotting James, the coward dropped its prey and took off.

"James Weaver!" It was Ma calling from the porch. He pretended to be too far away to hear. But Ma banged a rain bucket with the butter clapper. "James Weaver!"

He came back around the house, not too fast.

"Oh, thank the Lord thee's here. James, go over to the field and bring me back some wild indigo. Little droopy clusters of yellow petals. Thee will spot them right away."

"Aw, Ma, picking flowers?"

"James, I don't believe I've seen it written in Scripture that men can't pick a posy now and then."

"But, Ma—"

"And pull them out by the roots, son, because we'll brew a tea of the roots for Rebecca."

"What in heaven's name for?"

"It cures fever, son. Lizbet swears by it."

Miz Lizbet. Somehow she'd been crowned queen. Knew everything. Last week she'd caught him in front of the looking glass, rubbing his fingers over the fifty thousand freckles that had burst out on his face since they'd come to Kansas.

"Would you like to know what to do for it?"

"For what?" He'd spun around, and she stood behind him with her arms folded across her waist.

"Freckles. Back where I've been, white ladies just hate

102

it when those ugly spots pop out on their faces. They rub a cut lemon over their cheeks, or buttermilk with fresh green mint crushed in it."

"Disgusting." James savagely wiped at his face, as if to tear the freckles—or buttermilk—off.

"But I've got another idea, Mr. James Weaver, something that never fails, ever."

"Something that's not either lemons or buttermilk?"

"Oh yes, very different." She started busying herself, as if she'd forgotten what she was about to say, sweeping the infernal dust that always blew into the house.

"What is it?"

"What's what?"

"That never fails, Miz Lizbet."

"Oh, that." She pointed the handle of the broom at him, like Miss Malone's hickory stick. "I'll tell you, but you've got to do it once a week. You won't notice a big change the first week or two."

"What do I do?" James turned back to the looking glass, imagining his face white again, or better still, covered with a beard the color of an Irish setter. Then *her* face loomed in the glass from behind him.

"You take a nice thin layer of fresh cow manure—"

"Oh," James cried, running out of the house. But she called after him, "Put that on every week, and in two or three months, your face will be as clear as a baby's behind."

And now he was off to the field on another one of Miz Lizbet's harebrained schemes.

Ma brewed the wild indigo tea, which stunk something awful, while Miz Lizbet washed Rebecca in cool spring-water. She'd do one arm, dry it, lay it gently under the sheet, then the other arm; one foot, the other foot. Rebecca shivered, even as hot as it was in the house. The clattering of her teeth unnerved James as he tried to do his numbers. Algebra, they called it. Well, they might as well have called it gibberish. By fall, he'd have to be up with Jeremy and them on this mysterious stuff, but Lord only knew how. Maybe he'd make it if he worked enough of these wretched problems on his own over the summer.

Now Ma was blowing on the tea to cool it. She poured spoonfuls into Rebecca's mouth, while Miz Lizbet dabbed at the dribbles.

James turned back to his books, but then he heard this faint little wail, "I want James."

Oh no! What would he say to her? It was woman's work to tend to the sick, his to learn the infernal mathematics.

"James, thy sister's calling thee." Ma jerked her head, summoning him.

Rebecca's voice was faint as a distant cowbell, and he put his ear up to her lips. "James, am I going to die?"

Die? Only old people died. "Don't be stupid—"

But she cut him off. "Because if I am, I don't want thee to move into my room. Thee's far too messy."

"Well, in case no one's told thee, thy hair looks like a rat's nest right now." He glanced at Ma and saw a smile break through her worry mask.

"Does not, either."

"Does too!"

"Here, child, a bit more tea." Ma put the cooled cup to Rebecca's lips.

"Make James drink it first," Rebecca said.

"Not from thy cup."

Miz Lizbet jumped up and poured a steaming cup of the tea for James. She handed it to him with a smirk, as though it were a poisoned chalice. The tea roiled in the cup and smelled like wilted dandelions. Drink this? Not on his life!

"It won't hurt thee, son."

"If I hafta, he hasta," Rebecca said weakly, and so he took a sip. Burned his tongue.

Suddenly he reeled backward, tea sloshing everywhere. Miz Lizbet caught the china cup before it hit the floor. "Augggggh!" he wailed. "I'm dead."

"Not yet," Ma said. "Not until thee mops up the spill."

But Rebecca was laughing. "Can I have some more please, Ma?"

James was itching to know more about Matthew Luke Charles, the man with three first names, but he was wise to Miz Lizbet's game: You get more information if you act like you don't want any.

She was stirring a cauldron of water to boil Rebecca's sickbed linens. She hummed a throaty tune, and James was sure she was ready to burst with the story, so he said, "I'm going outside. There's a pile of logs that wants splitting."

"My Matthew Luke Charles, he could split a log faster than a bolt of lightning."

"Well, I don't work as fast, and Pa will be looking for the woodpile to grow soon."

"It's about 120 degrees out there. I don't think Mr.

Weaver's going to be laying a fire before the week's out. Down in Kentucky, we hardly ever needed a fire. Had a fireplace in our own house, too."

James opened the door, and Miz Lizbet came sailing across the room and slapped her hand down on his.

"Didn't your mama teach you not to walk out when somebody's talking to you?"

James affected a bored sigh and sank into Pa's rocker. "Go on," he said, as though she'd be reading to him from a seed catalog.

Miz Lizbet returned to the cauldron, her back to James. "He had it good for a while. Mr. Charles Senior took my Matthew Luke into the house, treated him like a real son. He had no other sons, you see, just two pimply-faced daughters who didn't have a mind for anything but their hoopskirts and their skin cremes. Anyway, Matthew Luke was his true son. He was smart, smart as a college man. He and his daddy ran the tobacco plantation. It got so Mr. Charles Senior didn't eat his morning grits without Matthew Luke telling him when to."

James rocked, pretending only mild interest. He fiddled with Ma's copy of *Godey's* magazine, half wondering what in blazes Ma found so fascinating.

"Well, Matthew Luke fancied me; I don't know why. I was just like every other field girl, with tobacco stains on my fingers from the picking. But somehow, it was me he liked." She spun around. "Bet that surprises you, because you think I'm an ugly old woman."

"Thee's not old," James said.

"Twenty-three," Miz Lizbet said sadly, as though she were crying over lost years. But she snapped out of it.

"Well, so we got married, and Mr. Charles Senior gave us the cottage out behind the plantation house. Guesthouse, he called it, only we were family, not guests. I lived there like a lady." She dunked a limp sheet into the cauldron and stirred until it disappeared into the water.

"But things turned around. Mr. Charles Senior, well, he died."

James leaned forward. "How?"

"Strangled in his sleep."

"Does thee know who did it?"

"Yes."

Well? Only silence. What a maddening woman! Was it time to threaten to go outside again? Then, suddenly Miz Lizbet seemed eager to finish the story, and she raced downhill through the rest.

"People said Matthew Luke strangled his daddy, for the money. It wasn't Matthew Luke. It was a dumb, half-blind old slave who got crazy on blackberry wine and squeezed the life out of Mr. Charles Senior on a dare."

James stilled the rocker, so as not to miss a single word.

"But Mrs. Charles Senior just had to believe Matthew Luke did it. She always hated him, because of who his mama was. She waited a decent time, then told the slaves that Matthew Luke had been tried and convicted in a court of law, and that it'd been left to her to see that justice was done. She called up three slaves who had a good eye for shooting ducks, and she gave them each a rifle, and she said they were a firing squad, duly appointed by the United States government."

James held his breath.

"And I didn't know it until I heard three gunshots all at once. After that, I took off running, and I've been running ever since. But not alone, no sir, James Weaver, I always take somebody with me, somebody who's wanting to make free."

CHAPTER NINETEEN

Plumb Crazy

July 1856

There was word of cattle coming through again, a herd of some two thousand longhorns driven up from Texas to the stockyards in Kansas City. Dairy farmers weren't too happy about it. They said, "Sure, the livestock will sell a lot dearer after they've had a few weeks of fattening up on our Kansas grass, free of charge. Gnaw it down until there's nothing left for our cows."

"Wait until you see these critters," Will said. "Big huge beasts, weigh about a ton, horns here to here, maybe four foot across. They're too sturdy to ever die, at least till they hit the slaughterhouse, and then, *bam*." He made a throat-slitting motion.

Jeremy added, "But they carry ticks that cause Texas fever. Our poor little old lonely cows out here, they pick up the Texas fever, and Lordy it's a sight to see 'em. Before long you'll see a cow or a bull going plumb crazy."

"That's something to look forward to," James said. He and Will and Jeremy perched on a fence at the south end of town, watching the cowboys drive the hundreds of cattle over the dusty trail.

Waving to them, Will asked, "Wouldn't you just die to be a cowboy?"

"Bet they never have freckles," James muttered, wrinkling up his nose.

The cowhands herded the cattle through a field where a few sleepy cows watched the parade. In the middle of the pasture, they were let to graze and slurp from the stream that greened the field.

"Except for the cow slobber, I could be a cowboy tomorrow," Will said dreamily.

"You'd be trampled in a mad stampede before morning," Jeremy said. "We'd pick you up flat as a buffalo chip. The Injuns could use you to light a fire. How about you, what do you want to be, James?"

Well, what could he say? The only thing he absolutely loved with a passion was drawing pictures of buildings. But boys didn't grow up into men who drew houses. "I expect I'll turn out a farmer."

"You going to grow Boston beans?"

"A doctor, then." He thought of the runt Dr. Olney, and then of Solomon and Thunder being led behind that slave catcher.

Will said, "At least being a doctor you'd get to see lots of ladies without their clothes on."

Jeremy asked, "But could you cut anybody open and pull out his guts?"

James's stomach flip-flopped. "An architect. I could build houses and hotels. They're going to need people to build up this big old prairie." And then he knew he'd accidentally hit on the right answer. He scanned the flat prairie all around them, the field hosting the snarling cattle, and he imagined buildings gently rising from the grass, not like in Boston—all those cold, gray towers, like the Howard Atheneum Theatre with its peaked roof jutting into the sky. No, the buildings he saw in his mind's eye now almost hovered over the flat land, with long, low windows stretching end to end, and porches ringing the house to capture the morning breeze on the south, the evening breeze from the north. What he saw were houses no one had ever seen before. Did he need algebra to build such wonders?

"Cowboy's better," Jeremy said, and Will added, "Me, as soon as my Pa'll let me, I'm going off to be a Jayhawker. I'll get me some of them red leggings and a musket to sling over my shoulder, and I'll kill me a hundred Border Ruffians. Look for me in the history books someday, hey?"

All his chores done, James walked into town to see how the new Free-State Hotel was coming along. They said it would cost $80,000 to rebuild it. They said the Eldridge brothers were putting up the money, and after it was done, the town would rechristen it the Eldridge Hotel, which was only fair. He watched a man hauling barrels of hot tar up to the roof, the acrid smell reminding him of Boston. Now, if he were designing this building, he'd put a little balcony off of each street-side room, and the front door would be as huge as the gateway to a palace. Or would that be out of proportion? He still had lots to learn since he'd made up his mind to be an architect.

Now he started for home, because Ma was planning an early dinner before she went off to the literary society meeting where they were discussing that new book of poetry she was always quoting from, something called *Leaves of Grass*. Pa would tease, "Why, Mrs. Weaver, that's a right secular book," but Ma would be ready with a comeback:

"Yes, Mr. Weaver, but it's full of the spirit God has emplanted within each of us. And when's the last time *thee* read a book?"

Two blocks from the hotel, James ran into Jeremy, bounding down the stairs from Bethany Maxwell's house.

"Oh, James, I was just stopping by to—to—"

"Knock her over with thy slobbery kisses?"

"Get my speller back."

"Um hm." James pantomimed looking high and low. "I don't see that blue-black speller in thy hand, friend."

"Well, I—"

And then, thank heaven, a glorious distraction! Staggering like a drunk came a boney old bull, weaving right down the main street.

"Didn't I warn you?" Jeremy said. "Texas fever, for sure."

The bull seemed delirious, panting and thrashing to and fro, its back arched, its head drooping nearly into the dust. Then the poor bull threw its head back, and James saw its glassy stare, its pain and confusion. It threw a fit and tossed its head so violently that it cracked its horn on the side of a wagon. A scream came out of the beast that sounded like the trumpeting of an elephant, which James had once heard in a circus.

By now a crowd was gathering—women wanting to help, children clinging to their mothers' skirts, dogs sniffing the dirt where the bull had been.

Then Bethany's father came out, pointing a rifle. "Stand back, y'all," he said, and lining himself up just so, he shot the bull right between the eyes.

As the bull fell to the ground, James wondered whether he would have had the courage to do the same thing, if he'd had the gun. Would he have been kind enough to put that bull out of its misery? Or courageous enough to protect his neighbors from that wild animal?

Or did it take more courage not to shoot?

CHAPTER TWENTY

Tornado!

The steady clip . . . clip . . . clip unnerved Dana, as the giant drops of thick summer rain hit the roof. The drops splashed into circles on the thirsty sidewalks. In a minute there would be a ferocious rumble as the rain gathered strength for its marathon. The radio was talking tornado.

". . . Right now, we're just under a watch, folks, but stay with us for updates. . . ."

Dana hated tornados, and not just because they were scary. She'd never lost a house or even so much as a bottle of nail polish in a tornado. Mostly she hated these storms because people in the Outside World thought of *Kansas* and *tornado* as interchangeable, as though all Kansans were extras from *The Wizard of Oz*.

The rain picked up now, cascading down the kitchen window like a waterfall. "Oh Auntie Em!" her cousin

Tonie always said when Dana visited her in California. "Oh Auntie Em, there's no place like home, there's *no* place like home!"

Then pellets fell from the sky, and in the ghoulish dark-in-the-day she saw balls of frozen rain ricochet off the cars parked on the street.

"Dingdong, the witch is dead, the witch is dead, the witch is dead," Tonie would sing in her obnoxious Munchkin voice. Dana turned up the radio.

". . . We're out here on the turnpike," the Voice of Weather crackled. "Can't see much for the blinding rain, but we sure can feel the hailstones bouncing off our van—wait a minute—there's an unconfirmed sighting . . . funnel cloud . . . the telltale hook . . . folks, this is the real thing!"

Dana switched stations. ". . . winds blowing at ninety-five miles per hour. If you don't have a basement, take cover in an inside hall, away from windows and any possible flying objects. . . ."

The tornado siren began its wail; the lights flickered. Dana grabbed a flashlight and her battery-operated radio and a bag of M&M's and ran down the stone steps to the basement. *Why did she have to be alone in the middle of a tornado?*

The basement was a gloomy canyon. Lightbulbs hung from the ceiling, casting a yellowish glare on the open wood studs that might someday support the walls of a classy poolroom. Now it all just looked raw and cavernous. The wind rumbled, thunder crashed, and the lightbulbs swayed. A three-legged table teetered and toppled as Dana bumped into it. Its chairs were piled lap-to-rear; she pulled one down to sit on and put her radio on another.

The flashlight threw an eerie circle on the stone shelves where Millicent Weaver must once have stored her vegetables and strips of dried pumpkin and salt pork. It wouldn't have been a basement then; cellar, they called it. Dana imagined Miz Lizbet Charles down here, her face as dark as the shadows. Maybe she hid some of the runaways here, with only candle glow to stab through the menacing darkness.

Dana shuddered, flipped through the radio dials looking for music. But there were only the frantic reports of mobile weather units. ". . . damage to a silo just west of . . . sighted a couple of cows hurled up against the side of a barn . . . the National Weather Service confirms reports of . . ." The voice went silent and was replaced by static. Dana changed stations. "Folks, if you're out in your car, don't try to outrun it. Abandon your car, find the nearest ditch or ravine. . . ."

A cold sweat chilled Dana, even in this stuffy basement. She put her hand to a damp wall and imagined that she was in a dungeon. Giveaway clothes that hung from a hook became carcasses—venison, pork, human. She thought of the bones of Lizbet Charles and wondered if the flesh had rotted from them in this basement before she was sealed in the room upstairs.

The radio crackled: "Breathe easier, folks, the National Weather Service tells us that the storm has passed over Lawrence and is headed for the Topeka area. We sustained only minimal damage, no reported deaths except for those two cows. Well, it sure shook us up. How about you, folks?"

Dana turned off the radio and scurried upstairs. She threw on all the lights to dispel the jaundiced look in the kitchen. Outside, the sun was trying to break through, as Dana surveyed the damage. There were tree branches piled everywhere. Cars pocked from the hail. A telephone cable hanging in the fir tree. Water rushing down the slope of Tennessee Street and forming a river at the bottom. A car inching through that river, splashing water over its roof.

Then the sun burst out—clear light in the peaceful silence after the storm, and the grass was suddenly a brilliant green. You had to squint to look at it.

Dana heard her cousin Tonie's voice in her head again: "Toto, I don't think we're in Kansas anymore."

"Ahn? Were you scared to death?"

Ahn's voice came through the phone thin and tremulous. "Oh Dana. My sisters and I crawled into bed and covered our heads until the storm was over. So scared!"

"Oh, you get used to it," Dana said casually. She'd never let Ahn know how terrified she'd been down in the basement alone. She thought of the carcasses, the damp stone wall. "I kept thinking what was it like for *them*."

"Millicent and Caleb and James and Rebecca?"

"Imagine this kind of storm over the open prairie. No trees, no shelter, no radios."

Ahn whispered, "Oh Dana, what if Miz Lizbet was up in that room when the storm came. Maybe she died of fright."

117

"Not her. I don't think she was afraid of anything. Remember how the journal says she left in the middle of the night for Missouri to bring out some more slaves? Think of it. A woman alone. I mean, I wouldn't even go down to Massachusetts Street alone at night. And a runaway at that, with all those nasty slave catchers out looking for slaves to sell back to the old masters."

"And Indians," Ahn said, for she'd just learned about all the Native Americans that had roamed the prairies, and she'd practiced pronouncing the strange names—Pawnee, Sioux, Kansa, Potawatomi.

"And don't forget the buffalo. How on earth did Miz Lizbet ever make it?"

Ahn's voice grew hard now: "People survive."

"But how did she live?"

"More interesting," Ahn said, "how did she die?"

CHAPTER TWENTY-ONE

Wild Indigo

August 1856

James cleaned the ashes out of the fireplace. "Thee's been promising since June," his mother reminded him. Rebecca slept hunched in the rocker, still weak after her bout with the fever. Seemed like everyone was sick. They had it over at the Macons', and even Governor Robinson, who the proslavers said *wasn't* the governor, was down with it. In town people were whispering "cholera," and talking about the epidemic that swept through here not ten years before, wiping out whites and Negroes and Indians alike.

But the runty Dr. Olney said, "Thee's got nothing to stew about, folks. Believe me, I'm a product of the Harvard Medical College. It's just the simple ague going around now." He gave everyone quinine and told them to sleep and sweat it away. Tonight, when he'd come to check on Rebecca, he'd said, "She's out of the woods. She's over the crest."

Ma said, "Praise the good Lord."

"Yes sir, the child's come through the dark of the night. She's turned the corner. We're seeing the light at the end of the tunnel. I tell thee, that quinine's a miracle drug. Wish I had the patent."

"I know thee has many calls to make tonight, and that sweet baby to get home to," Ma said, urging him toward the door. She never mentioned the wild indigo tea, but he was barely out to the road when Miz Lizbet said with a snort, "Quinine, my left elbow! It was the roots did it."

Now Ma and Miz Lizbet sat at the table, working on Lizbet's reading. She labored with writing the letters, because she was left-handed, and Ma could only show her how to work the right-handed way.

It gave James a hearty satisfaction to see Miz Lizbet struggling.

"I'll never get it, Miz Weaver."

"Nonsense." Ma stood up behind her and tried to guide her hand. "Maybe this is why thee has such a struggle sewing," Ma said with a sigh.

"Should never have been *G*s invented," Miz Lizbet muttered. "Too fancy and curly to write."

James stuck his head back into the chimney, and felt drops. "It's raining. I sure can't sweep up wet ashes."

"Work quickly, before they turn to mud," Ma said. "And save every bit of the ash, son, because I'll be leaching it in the fall and using the lye to make my soap."

In Boston they'd bought soap, fragrant as violets. Out

here, Mrs. Macon was teaching Ma to make her own soap. A brown crock stood at the back of the stove, and into it went every drop of fat Ma could save. James couldn't imagine washing in anything made from ashes and lard. How do you get clean when you smell like a pig?

"The rain better stop," Miz Lizbet said, "because I'm going on tonight."

James bumped his head on the stone in his excitement. Finally! He looked up and saw Ma's disapproving eyes.

"It's threatening a storm, child."

Miz Lizbet slammed her copybook shut. "I have to leave tonight. Folks are expecting me."

"Thee will catch thy death," Ma said, flattening the copybook open again. "Now, watch here. Thy *O*s must be as round as tiny moons."

"The minute it gets dark," Miz Lizbet said. "My rucksack's all packed."

"I urge thee to reconsider."

She shook her head. "There's good moonlight to guide me, Miz Weaver, trusting the storm doesn't cover it up, and by the time I get to those folks down in Missouri, there will be only a sliver of moon, so our trip back here will be safe."

"But, Lizbet—"

"Amen," she said firmly.

It wasn't just one wagon or two. It was a whole train of them that James watched come over the hill, looking like they'd fall headfirst into a ravine. Their white covers billowed in the Kansas wind like sails on the open sea. In fact, folks were calling these wagons prairie schooners. And they were headed right for the middle of town.

James walked alongside the wagons and the beat-up-looking oxen that pulled them. Plumb in the middle of Massachusetts Street, the lead wagon stopped, all the others waiting behind like obedient ducklings.

People began to tumble out of the wagons, stretching and yawning and turning their faces toward the sun. A rumpled-looking man bumped right into James. "Lawd, I never expected to stop in such a pretty town. This is just about the Garden of Eden."

"I expect thee's been traveling a good long while, if thee thinks that!"

"'Thee?' What are you, a Bible person?"

"Quaker, sir. We're Friends."

"Well sure we're friends. Molly, hon, come over here and meet my new young friend."

Molly waddled from around the other side of the wagon. She proved to be a woman fixing to burst. James figured Lawrence would be adding one more name to its rolls before the day was out.

"You got a doctor here?" Molly growled.

"Yes, ma'am. Dr. Olney and Dr. Robinson, both, but Dr. Robinson's usually away on government business."

"Best you be going for Dr. Olney," the woman said, holding on to her heaving belly.

Heart pounding, James ran for Dr. Olney's house. "Dr. Olney, sir, there's a woman over by the hotel who's about to foal. Better come."

James led the doctor through the maze of wagons to

Molly, who was as pale as the cover on the wagon, and clutching its ropes. Dr. Olney helped her up to the wagon, and they disappeared inside, while Molly's husband paced.

"I may look old, but I sure never had a baby before," he told James. "Molly, she's a good sport. She wanted to come along for the ride to Oregon, so I married her proper, after fifty-some years as a bachelor."

James meant to listen as the man, who called himself Jed Pryor, revealed fifty years of his personal history. But James's attention was drawn to the house across the street—Bethany Maxwell's house. Mr. Maxwell propped his door open and began carrying out trunks and boxes and barrels. One trip, he had a one-hundred-pound sack of flour flung over his back like a dead body. And he was loading everything onto one of the wagons.

Then Bethany came out, with her cat curled in her arms. "Oh, hello, James Weaver."

"Is thy pa leaving?"

"All of us," she said morosely. She buried her face in the black fur of the cat.

James swallowed around a lump the size of a goose egg.

"My mother says no more. No more warring and no more bleeding Kansas and no more flooding, and no more lightning and thunder."

"Where's thee going?" James asked, thunderstruck himself by how Bethany Maxwell's hair was just the color of the cat's fur, and her eyes like early dusk.

"My Uncle Louis has come for us, from Cincinnati. We're following the Oregon Trail."

"Thee's bound for adventure," James said bravely.

"But it's clear over the other side of the mountains. And I can't take Trembles. You could keep him for me." She thrust the cat into James's arms. "He's an outside cat. He won't scratch at your door or anything rude like that."

Trembles scurried out of James's grasp and wound himself around Bethany's leg. She tried to ignore him. "We're sleeping in the wagon tonight and leaving at first light." She picked up a small satchel her father had left on the porch. "I can't take much."

What was he supposed to say? Certainly not *I'm gonna shrivel up and die without thee,* though he suspected he might do just that.

"I'll remember you, James, over on the other side of the mountain, because I never met anybody who said 'thee' and 'thy' before."

"I can say 'you' and 'your.'"

"No, don't! Now, take Trembles or I'll cry right here on the street." She slid away from the cat, and James grabbed him up and ran home.

It wasn't until he was inside with Trembles that he wondered just what kind of baby Molly and Jed Pryor would be taking the rest of the way on the Oregon Trail.

Pa pulled off his traveling boots. "It's so far from place to place out here," he said, settling into the biggest chair on the porch. "Thought I'd not make it home to sleep in my own bed tonight."

"Ma misses thee when thee's gone away on business," James said.

Trembles came around the corner and hissed at Pa.

"Who's this?"

"Just a cat. The Maxwells left him in our keeping. They went off to Oregon, while you were away." James fiddled with a knife and a stick, making it look like he was idly whittling strips off the cottonwood branch, when he was actually carving little figures in it. If it turned out all right, he'd give it to Pa for a letter opener. And if it didn't turn out all right, he could use it to stir up anthills.

Ma brought them out some lemonade. "Hush thy voices so Rebecca doesn't hear and clamber out of bed. I'm afraid we've spoiled her fiercely through her illness."

"I trust Simon Olney was a help?"

"Oh yes," Ma said quickly. "Came out three times." Not a word about Miz Lizbet's wild indigo tea. "The man is a veritable symphony of hackneyed expressions. He pronounced our Rebecca fit as a fiddle, tight as a drum, and snug as a bug in a rug."

Pa laughed as he polished his scuffed boots.

This was James's favorite time of the day, when the daylight finally gave in to dusk, and the sun was just a memory, a ripple of soft purples on the horizon. Ten more minutes, and it would be too dark to carve without bloodying his fingers, or worse, making a mess of the scarce wood. He asked, "Pa, did thee find Solomon?"

"I did," Pa said, letting out a deep sigh. "They have a different interpretation of the law down there."

"Thee wasn't able to bring the man back?" asked Ma, taking up her knitting.

"Well, Mrs. Weaver, they can't deny I've got legal papers proving Solomon's a free man, but they surely can take a long time looking those papers over."

Ma's needles clicked furiously.

There came a clattering of wagon wheels from up out of the sunset, and Ma stuffed her knitting behind her and folded her hands in her lap. James felt his heart leap. Eight days had passed since Miz Lizbet had left in the storm. Was this her promised load of Negroes?

The wagon drew nearer, and James heard raucous laughter. He stood up to get a better look. One man held the reins, and the other stood up against the sunset and tilted a jug back toward his mouth. Wiping his face on his shirtsleeve, he shouted, "Ain't never seen a sunset like this since I come back from Gay Paree."

"Hell, you ain't never been to Paris," the driver said, yanking the jug away. He took a good long slug of the contents, too. James smiled to himself, imagining what it must feel like to be so freely drunk.

Pa muttered, "Scallywags. I'll go head them off," but Ma jumped up and said, "Caleb Weaver, this requires a woman's firm hand. I'll scold them as if I were their own mother. James, thee come out to greet them with me. He'll protect me, Mr. Weaver. Thee's had a long day of travel."

Pa seemed only too glad to sit back, as James followed Ma and her long swishing skirt down to the wagon.

The driver doffed his sweaty hat at Ma. "Evening, missus. Don't pay us no mind, we've been to the well." The other man thought this was hilarious, and he bellowed with laughter.

"Are thee drunk?" Ma hissed, snatching the jug away from the driver. She poured what was left on the ground.

"James, poke around in the back of the wagon," Ma said, and then the driver turned sober all of a sudden.

"You Miz Weaver?"

"I am."

"Well, I brought those bolts of cloth you ordered from down in Missouri. Real pretty calico. Gift from a Miz Charles."

"I simply can't accept the gift, sir, generous as it is. We're a proud people out here on the prairie."

James climbed carefully into the wagon, so as not to trample anything, or anyone. He lifted a corner of the buffalo robe and saw two eyes, which snapped shut right away. He jumped off the wagon.

Ma said, in a voice much louder than usual, "I don't mean to be inhospitable, but my husband's up on that porch, and he's weary from a day of travel, and I believe thee had best be on thy way. Perhaps someone further up the line can use that good cloth."

"Well, ma'am, I've got strict orders to deliver this load to you and no one but."

Ma came around to the far side of the wagon and whispered, "There's two walls of a soddy just up the road, beside a stream. Not much water, this time of the year, but enough to refresh the horses. Drive thy wagon about until thee sees all the lights go out in our house. Thee can stay the night there, but be gone by the first sun, hear?"

"Amen," came a voice from under the buffalo robe.

CHAPTER TWENTY-TWO

Hush Puppies

The whole gang waited for Jeep in front of the Eldridge Hotel at Seventh and Massachusetts. It was a sticky day, the kind where the sun hides behind weighty clouds.

"Whew, there's not even a breeze," Sally complained, fanning herself with a *Tiger Beat.*

Mike asked, "You guys want to go over to the quarry to swim?"

"Too hot to swim."

"Not without suits."

"Michael!"

Dana suggested, "We could go explore the old Edmund Wolcott Castle. It might be torn down by fall."

"Oh yeah," Derek said, "that's one of my personal favorite things to do—mess around a condemned build-ing, machete our way through spiderwebs, get busted for trespassing. Go for it!"

"No really, it's a cool place," Dana protested. "My dad's head of the committee to save Wolcott Castle."

"I'm impressed," Mike said. "Next idea?"

"The mall?" Sally offered.

"No money."

"No ride."

"No way."

Derek said, "How can summer be so short and so long at the same time?"

"Might as well enjoy it," Sally said. "Next year we'll all have to have jobs."

Ahn reminded them, "I already have a job. I cook for all my brothers and sisters, and that doesn't mean putting hot dogs in the microwave. Lots of chop-chopping."

"Do you get paid?"

"Of course I get paid. I get free room and board."

"We all do."

"But you have parents," Ahn said.

Finally, Jeep's dad let him out in front of the hotel, with his two little brothers who were about six and eight. "I had to baby-sit," he grumbled.

"We're not babies."

"They can't even zip their own pants," Jeep said, at which point, of course, all the guys checked their flies.

"Why is it girls never forget to zip up, and guys always do?" Dana asked.

"That's a sexist remark."

"Derek takes offense, tsk tsk," Dana clucked. "We sure haven't seen you around much, Jeep."

"Hey, you're just my white friends," he said, grinning. "Most of the time I hang out with the brothers."

"That's us!" Calvin and Luther cried.

"Not you, armpits. I mean the guys from church. And besides, I've been over at the KU library a lot."

"*You* go to the library during summer vacation?" Derek said. "Geez."

"Calvin, jump on his face, will you?" Jeep's brother was only too glad to accommodate, leaping and glomming onto Derek's neck like a chimp.

"I can't breathe!"

Jeep peeled the kid off and threw his arm around Calvin's neck as if he were holding him hostage. "I've been studying up on things. I might just end up smart, or an FBI man."

"Let's not stand here like idiots," Mike suggested. "Let's go eat."

"Yeah, because what I've got to tell you needs to be heard when you're stuffing your faces." Jeep glanced up and down the street. "How about Long John Silver's? Oh yeah!" he added, under his breath.

Whoever had money kicked in two or three dollars so they could order a family-sized Fish 'n More, and all six of them crowded into one booth. Naturally Calvin and Luther were banished to another table, where the first thing they did was loosen the lids on all the salt-and-pepper and sugar shakers and the malt vinegar bottle.

When the order came, Jeep waited until Derek's mouth was stuffed.

"What's that you're eating, man?"

"This?" He pulled the whole ball out of his mouth and studied it.

"You're a pig!" Sally said.

"It's a hush puppy," Derek said, popping it back in his mouth.

"That's what I thought. Okay, this man up in Iowa? Long time ago? He was a church deacon, named Theron Trowbridge. Calvin, stop tearing open all those straws, unless you're planning to have 'em all stuffed up your nose. Anyway, this guy Theron used to let runaway slaves stay at his house all the time. See, the poor fools would run off with no particular place to go, just following the drinking gourd—"

"The North Star," Dana translated.

"—and those slave hunters who got money for bringing back the runaways? They'd get bloodhounds on the trail, see. Well, sometimes the runaways would just jump in a river to put the dogs off their scent. But up near old Theron's place, there wasn't even a creek. It was as dry as your bathtub, Derek."

"Get to the point." Derek was growing impatient, and besides, he reminded them that the $1.50 movie would be starting in twenty minutes.

"Okay, okay. Anyway, old Theron—Luther, don't you pull that life preserver off the wall, or I'm throwing you to the sharks—Theron used to feed those bloodhounds."

"What a traitor!" cried Ahn.

"But wait. He fed them corn dodgers."

Sally asked, "What are those?"

"Well, they're like, sort of like balls of fried cornmeal."

"Like we're eating," Mike said.

"Yeah, right. Only Theron spiced them up good—with strychnine. In a minute, those dogs were dead meat. And you know what Theron called the corn dodgers?"

"Don't tell me, let me guess," Dana said. "Hush puppies?"

Mike gasped and spit a mouthful of soggy mush across the table.

"Eat hearty!" Jeep said merrily.

After the movie, at Pennie Annie's soda shop, Jeep told them about the typhoid fever. "Everybody in town had it in 1856 or '57, because the whole place was like a pigsty, and they drank raw milk hot out of the cow, and as soon as one person picked up the bug, voom, he passed it right along."

Sally said, "Like the flu we all got last winter. I swear, I coughed for two months."

"Except for one little difference. You survived. This typhoid stuff killed people. It's how Miz Lizbet Charles died," Jeep said. "I'm so sure that I'd lay my brothers' lives down for it."

"Hey!" Calvin yelled.

"But I can't figure out how she got walled into that room."

Mike jumped in with, "We can develop a bunch of grotesque theories, though. Starting with—savage Indians."

"You've seen too many movies," Dana said. "Indians are never once mentioned in the journal, and anyway the Delawares around here were friendly and peaceful."

"No Indians. Okay. Murder! Let's say, somebody's dying of the typhoid thing, and he wants Miz Lizbet dead for some reason, so he opens a vein and squirts blood into Lizbet's eye—"

Sally sucked to the screechy part of her Coke. "You know how boring you guys are? That's all you ever talk

132

about anymore—slaves and dead bodies, and now dead dogs. I mean really, squirting blood into the poor woman's eye?"

"Sally's right," Mike said. "Let's declare a truce. No more talking about the skeletal remains of any unknown parties, as found in Dana's house, until school starts."

"Two months?" Ahn protested.

"Okay, until the Fourth of July," Mike conceded.

That would give Dana a few more weeks—enough time to solve the mystery—and besides, she'd promised to give up the diary at the beginning of July. Suddenly she noticed that everyone was waiting for her to say something.

Mike said, "We've all agreed except you. You're the keeper of the bones."

"July Fourth," Dana agreed, nodding.

They all crisscrossed their straws on the table. A pact.

CHAPTER TWENTY-THREE

Will's Quest

September 1856

When James opened the door, he was surprised to see Will all geared up for who-knows-what. He was wearing those new Levi Strauss blue trousers, and red leggings, and around his waist—a leather belt with a gun pulling one side low. "Just came to say good-bye, James."

James stuffed his hands into his pockets, as if he could reach in and pull out the right words to say.

"I'm heading over by Osawatomie, to see if I can find John Brown and his men, or else I'll join up with Lane's Army, whichever I get to first, or whichever's got those proslavery ruffians in the crosshairs of their rifles." Will shifted his feet, stared him down, no doubt waiting for James to praise either his getup or his valor.

"Well, I wish thee luck," James said lamely.

Will seemed irked, as if saying "good luck" wasn't

enough. "I might not come back, you know. Or I might come back in a box."

James nodded.

Will pulled the gun out of the holster and twirled it. James recoiled as he might if a rattlesnake actually lunged for him. But he recovered enough to say, "Go in peace, friend."

"Oh mercy, Weaver, have you got it all wrong!"

"I s'pose that's possible."

But then Will grinned, flipped the gun to his left hand, and stuck his right one out for James to shake. James pulled his hand out of his pocket so slow, as if he were drawing it through quicksand.

"I'll see ya when the cows come home," Will said, and he ran off down the road, his gun flapping against his hip.

That night James asked, "Pa, what do you say to a violent man about nonviolence?" What he really meant was, *what ought I to have said to Will?*

"Thy mother's the preacher in the family. I'm just a God-fearing man practices the law."

"Yes, Pa." James knew more was coming, because Pa never could resist summing up before the jury.

"But I reckon I'd say to such a man, the good Lord tells us to love one another, to do unto others, and in plain black and white, not to kill another living being."

"Yes sir, but there's this man John Brown everyone's talking about."

"A barbarian," Pa said with a sneer.

"Yes sir, but Miss Malone says *he's* a God-fearing man, dead set against slavery, because the Bible says to be."

"Mark my words, the man's a fanatic. No good will come of his swashbuckling."

"But Pa, at least he's on the right side."

Pa came the closest to exploding that James had ever witnessed. He slammed a book down on the table, knocking the lantern to the floor. James watched in horror as a vein at Pa's temple throbbed like a heartbeat. "How can you be on the right side, if you do violence to another human being? Some do God's work in silent dignity."

Ma! Did he know?

A long time passed, James sitting absolutely still. Then Ma came in with Rebecca, and each had a handful of sunflowers taller than Rebecca.

"You mean to thatch our roof with those?" Pa asked—a joke without a hint of humor in his tone.

"No, Mr. Weaver, I aim to get sunflower oil from these."

"And we're going to pull out the seeds and dry them and eat them like nutmeats all winter," Rebecca said. "If we have too much food, we'll put them out for the squirrels."

Ma must have noticed the strain on James's face, and she flashed him a question: *Miz Lizbet?*

He quickly responded. "Will's gone off to fight with John Brown or Jim Lane, one."

"I see." Ma's voice was as hard as a kernel of corn. "Rebecca, take these sunflowers down to the cellar for now. Run along."

"How come I always have to run along whenever Ma says 'I see' just that way?"

Pa pointed straight toward the cellar door. Rebecca made a point of tripping over his feet on her way to the cellar, but Pa didn't even reach out to steady her.

"Well, I guess I'd best sit down," Ma said, backing into her rocker.

"The boy's asking about how we should act in the face of violence."

"I didn't know what to say to Will, Ma." Ma reached out and patted his neck, and he felt himself blush. He couldn't wait until he had a beard so no one could see his blushing.

"Back in Worcester, Massachusetts," Pa began, "there came a slave catcher to town one day. I was there working on a case involving a Friend, an abolitionist who'd been brought up on charges for harboring runaway slaves." He fixed his eyes on Ma, who turned away.

He knows, James thought.

"Well, what to do, what to do? This man was a filthy, immoral outhouse rat. He didn't care about human beings, only about the bounty on the heads of the freed men. Well, half the men in Worcester wanted to rip this scoundrel apart, throw him into the river in a thousand pieces."

"Oh Lord," Ma cried, her hand clapped to her mouth.

"But the Good Book says we must do what God expects of us. We called a gathering at the Meeting House."

A bunch of Quakers, deciding the whole thing in silence, James thought to himself, and a smile stole out of the corners of his mouth.

"No need to smirk, James, listen to thy father."

"Yes, ma'am."

"Talked it all out, we did, and it was decided how we'd respond. A swarm of us surrounded the man, fastened our indignation on his face, followed him around every minute of the day. He didn't have a minute to relieve himself, without we were right there beside him. And we never made a threat."

"So what happened?" asked James.

"Well, on the third night we let our guard down, and some men of a different persuasion—I'm not talking proslavers, son, I'm talking 'godly' men, like your John Brown—they pulled this vermin up out of his bed, and beat him up until he could hardly stand on his two feet."

Something inside James yearned to cheer, before he felt a lump of supper rise in his throat.

"And then, Mr. Weaver?" Ma asked quietly. Not even her knitting needles clicked.

"Well, we took the man over to the Meeting House, and we nursed him back to health, and when he could walk on his own, why the whole band of us Friends, we surrounded him again and got him safely on the train out of town. Do you understand, son?"

"Yes sir," he said, then, "No sir," with a twinge of fear in his heart.

"Well, thy mother and I pray that thee will, if thee's tested."

Light flooded James's bedroom, so bright it woke him in the middle of a wondrous dream. There was enough light for it to be high noon, and yet James saw midnight black at the edges of the light.

Fire!

He jumped out of bed, yelling, "Pa, Pa, it's burning out there!"

Pa had already pulled on his trousers by the time James got downstairs. Ma, her hair flying around her face, was collecting buckets and kettles.

"Take 'em outside to the pump," Pa yelled, "and pump for all thee's worth."

James looked up to see Rebecca at the top of the stairs, trailing her blanket.

Ma snapped, "Child, wrap up in thy blanket and get thee out behind the house."

"Oh no, another fire?" Rebecca whined.

"It's a prairie fire," Pa explained, fastening his boots. "It'll not touch our house, if all the neighbors work quickly, and the wind's kind. Do as thy mother says."

Out back, James pumped water as fast as he could, watching the flames on the horizon leap toward the moon. He saw their neighbors in the distance, silhouetted against the flames, human chains tossing buckets of water on the fury of the fire. The ones in front rotated to the back when the heat got too intense.

The night was bursting with noise: The crackling of the dry autumn grass; the frantic yells—"Faster! More water"; howling flames sucking the air around them; cattle stampeding right into the flames; crying babies, wailing men who'd become pillars of fire.

No time to think, no time to react. *Just keep the water*

coming. James ran toward the flame, with six buckets slung across a shoulder pole. The water sloshed out, and he was drenched. Next trip, he'd carry only four buckets. He could run faster and not lose as much water.

"Hurry!" the men yelled, and James sped up.

Now Ma and Pa and all the able-bodied people of Lawrence were running with buckets and kettles. The women soaked blankets in washtubs and passed them to the men up close to beat out the flames. Some were overcome with smoke or plain exhaustion, and the women and children dragged their menfolk away to safety.

An old hand on the prairie recommended that they build a backfire, which made no sense at all to James until he remembered Grampa Baylor saying, "Thee must fight fire with fire, James." It took forever until the two fires met and leaped twenty, thirty feet into the air. Another hour or two passed before it was all under control, just about the time the sun was beginning to turn the sky the color of flame again.

But the air was black with smoke and soot from the two houses that had been in the path when the flames jumped Quail Feather Creek. The air was thick enough to grab by the handful. People began to stumble home, murmuring reassuring words to one another. In the morning, after some rest, they'd assess the damages, clean up, count their cattle.

James tumbled back into bed with his boots still on. He turned his sheets wet and black, but he was asleep in a minute and barely noticed when Rebecca slid in beside him.

"James?"

"Phmph?"

"Was thee a hero out there?"

"Hush up and let me sleep." He drifted peacefully downward—and heard a small voice, as though it came from the far reaches of the open prairie.

"Was thee scared?"

James could make his voice say these words, without opening his eyes, almost without moving his lips. "Rebecca, thee must learn to fight fire with fire. That's all there is to it."

CHAPTER TWENTY-FOUR

J'm Melting, J'm Melting!

Dana's summer was twirling away like smoke from a chimney, wasted and directionless. She and her mother peeled wallpaper from another room (no bodies hidden there), and Dana helped with mailings for the Save Wolcott Castle campaign, which her father had taken up with a driving vengeance.

But with the kids, it just wasn't the same. When she saw Mike or Derek or Ahn, this thing about not mentioning Lizbet Charles grew and grew and filled the space with unspeakable emptiness. She remembered someone on TV once saying, "Whatever you do, don't think of pink elephants," and then, of course, that's all you could think of.

Dana's house was headquarters for Save Wolcott Castle. Each spare room was filled with posters, computer print-outs, stamps, envelopes, and government documents.

"Aw, Dad, why can't I sneak in and see the house?" Dana asked.

Her father's answer was firm: "No way. It's too dangerous."

"But you've been in it."

"I have life insurance. Don't ask me again; it's out of the question until the restoration is well under way. *If* we raise the money."

With the big July Fourth fund-raiser coming up, no one really wanted to make the annual visit to the Shannon side of the family, but they had nonrefundable tickets, and so Dana and her parents went to southern California.

Her least favorite relative was her cousin Tonie, the snob, who'd be a freshman in the fall. Tonie thought Kansas was a laugh riot ("People really *live* there?"), and she had her usual *Wizard of Oz* stuff to goad Dana with.

At Disneyland, while they were waiting to get into the Haunted Mansion, Dana stupidly said, "I hope it's worth all this standing in line in the boiling sun," to which Tonie (who weighed in at about 185 loosely assembled pounds) crumbled to her feet and wailed, "I'm melting! I'm melting!"

People dashed to her rescue, including a guy who said, "Let me through, I'm a veterinarian," but Dana reassured them. "Don't worry, she's just the Wicked Witch of the West."

"Next year," Dana's mother muttered on the way back to the airport, "we go to someplace more fun, like the Black Hole of Calcutta or the Bermuda Triangle."

On the plane, Dana reread Millicent Weaver's journal.

September 11, 1856—Our afternoons are pleasant, but there's a nip in the air in the mornings. I suppose the winter they warn us of will inevitably descend. Well, perhaps the harsh weather will keep Caleb home with us more, and the "traffic" through here less.

September 16, 1856—Caleb is off in Westport on constitution business again, but with the help of God, he's been able to free young Solomon from the clutches of that unscrupulous man in southern Missouri. Poor Solomon stumbled into our house last night, looking more like a crazed animal than a human being. Someone had mistaken him for a wolf, I surmise, and shot him. The bullet passed right through the upper flesh of his arm and left a ghastly wound. Oh, dear Lord. He'd walked the whole way for nine nights, with no shoes, sleeping in haylofts when he dared, but mostly in open ditches. All that time he spoke to no one, for fear he'd be sent back, even with legal papers in his hand.

Millicent Weaver's words and the echoes of the past seemed more real to Dana than the otherworldly voices that floated above the engines' roar. A baby's wailing from somewhere in the back of the plane was stifled with a bottle, and Millicent continued her whispers across the century.

September 17, 1856—Miz Lizbet tends to Solomon, though he sleeps and sleeps. She bathes him like a baby and applies fresh poultices of purple prairie clover to his arm. I sent James after Dr. Olney, but Miz Lizbet was peeved and stopped him, saying, "I don't want that fool in here." Solomon's eyes fluttered open, and he said, "Dr. Olney's a good man, Miz Lizbet," and then he drifted off again. Miz Lizbet believes that tomorrow Solomon will be strong enough to send on home, for which I'm grateful, because Caleb's due home by suppertime, and Miz Lizbet must be getting on with her work elsewhere.

I believe she's sweet on Solomon.

Dana's mother slept through the whole plane ride. Being on her good behavior for a week with the in-laws always wore her out, but only spurred Dana's father into great productivity. From San Francisco to Denver, he scribbled notes for a paper he'd be giving at the end of the summer. Somewhere over the neat grid of western Kansas, he noticed what Dana was reading. The historian in him kicked in: "Is that the diary?"

"I guess it's time," she said, and she turned it over to him.

He pulled out the folding magnifying glass a good historian always carries, and he turned to page one.

The first ones have been here, and if Thou hast been with them, they are well on their way to Canada. . . .

Dana's father read to the very end of the journal, just before the twenty blank pages.

November 20, 1856—The letter from Mother was twelve days getting here. I pray Thou hast watched over Father through these days, and that Thou hast preserved his strength until Rebecca and I reach Boston. These are troubling times. My heart breaks to think that I might never get back here to Caleb and James. Therefore, I am leaving this diary with Lizbet, as it is her story more than mine.

He gave the journal back to Dana. "A treasure," he said simply.

"Can I make copies?"

"No, electronic copying isn't good for old documents. I guess you know that next week is the first of July."

"Yes," she said with a sigh. "I'm giving it to Dr. Baxi."

"I'm not sure I could give the journal up," her father said quietly. "Especially now that I know James Weaver as a twelve-year-old. In all the stuff going on about the house, I guess you never heard the name of the architect. James Baylor Weaver designed Wolcott Castle."

CHAPTER TWENTY-FIVE

All Alone

November 1856

"Oh mercy, here comes Mr. Weaver," Ma cried, and Miz Lizbet snatched up her shawl and ran up the stairs. At the top she called down, "Will he be all right?" She meant Solomon, who sat in Pa's chair, pasty and pale, with a lap robe about his knees.

"Well, I reckon I can take care of one Solomon," Ma said crossly. "Now thee must get up there, and for heaven's sake, don't utter a peep while Mr. Weaver's in the house. Rebecca!" Ma warned, fixing her with a stern scowl.

"Yes, Ma, I know."

"Solomon Jefferson, I needn't say anything to thee?"

"No, ma'am."

"And James?"

James stashed away a sketch of a building that reached

toward the sky. It would be higher than anything in Boston. "No, Ma. I've got good at lying."

"Not *lying*, exactly."

"Well, what would thee call it, Ma?"

"I'd call it doing God's will, James. Now hush." She tidied her hair in the looking glass and threw the door open just as Pa came up the porch steps. "Welcome home, Mr. Weaver."

Rebecca flew toward Pa, while James held back in a more manly fashion, but it sure was good to have Pa home.

After a minute, Ma stepped aside so Pa could see into the room.

"Is this Solomon? Well, fancy!" He went over to shake Solomon's hand.

"Mind, he's got a bad arm," Ma whispered. So Pa just smiled and said, "It's good to have thee back."

"Thank you, sir. Without you—"

"Thunder come back with thee?"

"No sir," he said, hanging his head.

"Small price to pay," Ma snapped, "for the piece of work that is a man."

"They've been looking after me a couple days, Mr. Weaver. I'll be heading over to Olneys' tomorrow."

"Well, we'll see," Ma said.

And then, as though he'd waited over in the old soddy out back until Pa was home, U.S. Marshal Fain loomed in the doorway. A smile spread across his craggy face as soon as he spotted Solomon. "Evening Mr. Weaver, Mrs. Weaver." He tipped his hat so all of them would notice the marshal's badge pinned to it. "I'm investigating a report that there's been some illegal Nigras hiding out—"

"In my house?" Pa asked.

"Well, nearby. Who's this?"

Solomon jumped to his feet, and Pa stepped back to put his arm around him.

"This is Solomon Jefferson, a free man. He works as a groomsman for Dr. Olney."

"Um hm. You wouldn't happen to have papers proving that, would you?"

"I do, sir." Solomon pulled some papers out of a leather pouch under the lap robe. He held the papers out, but the marshal wouldn't take them directly from him.

Finally, Ma snapped the papers out of Solomon's hands and waved them under the marshal's nose. "Does thee need me to read them to thee?"

"I can read good enough." He looked up with mean eyes like hard coffee beans. "Folks say there's a lot of mysterious comings and goings here, Miz Weaver."

Rebecca sidled over to James, who held her hand good and tight.

"Now listen here, Marshal," Pa said. "I am a man sworn to uphold the law. Like you," he said, but the irony was lost on Marshal Fain.

"Oh yes sir, Mr. Weaver, and it's also a matter of public record that you defended one Barnaby Watts, an abolitionist in clear disregard for the law of the land."

"There were legal grounds."

"And it's also a matter of public record that it's against the law to aid and abet Nigras when they're running off from their masters who legally and morally have dominion."

"The moral argument would be lost on thee, Mr. Fain."

Then Ma stepped forward, all sweetness and light. "Marshal, thee sees this man Solomon Jefferson. Does it follow that we might be hiding other Negroes if we've got Mr. Jefferson out here in plain sight?"

"I'm only saying, Miz Weaver—"

"Because gladly would I step aside and let thee search my house if thee suspects anything of the sort."

"Ma!" Rebecca cried.

"Has thee not made thy bed, child?"

James squeezed Rebecca's hand until he was afraid he'd crack a finger. "Ouch," she mumbled.

"Miz Weaver, I won't search your house."

"Not without a warrant, thee won't," Pa said.

"But it's mighty curious, Mr. Weaver, how you're scouting all around Kansas Territory defending lawbreaking abolitionists, writing a constitution which the president of the _U_-nited States himself says is illegal, that you're taking darkies away from their rightful masters"—he glared at Solomon—"and then you're saying you're a man of the law. Seems like you're blowing smoke out of two different chimneys, if you ask me."

"Good evening, Marshal Fain." Pa's words chilled the room.

"I believe we'll light a fire," Ma said, and she busied herself with kindling. "James, fetch us three sturdy logs. Thee can walk the marshal down to the road on thy way."

"No need," Marshal Fain said, turning on his heels. But then he said, "Nearly forgot. I've brought the missus out a letter from Boston. Hope it's not bad news."

* * *

"What is it, Millicent?" Pa said.

"My father. He's suffered a stroke." Ma held the letter to her heart.

"What's a stroke, Ma?" Rebecca asked.

"Something snaps in the brain, child, leaves a man unable to walk sometimes, or talk. Oh Lord, Caleb, I must get to Boston."

James couldn't imagine Grampa Baylor felled by anything, and certainly not reduced to a helpless stalk of a man. He remembered old Mr. Dunworthy in Boston, his body crooked to the left, just staring into empty air under a shade tree near Faneuil Hall. "Will Grampa's face be all twisted up, Ma?"

Pa was scanning the letter now. "No way to tell from what thy grandmother's written. Yes, Millicent, thee and Rebecca must leave at first light. It will be many days' travel, and best done before the truly cold weather sets in."

"It's nearly the end of November," Ma said, her voice childlike with unaccustomed fear. "We might not be back by Christmas."

But Pa was all business. "I can take thee by wagon to Leavenworth, where thee can get the stagecoach."

"We're going back to Boston!" Rebecca squealed.

Ma hushed her with the shake of a finger. "But what will become of thee, and of James?"

"We're perfectly capable of looking after ourselves, Mrs. Weaver." Pa sounded so sure, but James wondered if they *could* get along. Neither one of them had ever cooked an egg, much less a whole chicken. And what if some of Miz Lizbet's people came through? And Christmas without Rebecca or Ma was unthinkable.

"I'll be glad to stay and give 'em a hand," Solomon offered.

"We'll call upon thee if we need thee, sir, but I suspect, what with the typhoid fever going around, Dr. Olney will need thee worse."

James waved until he could no longer see the wagon, and when he went back to the house it seemed like an empty cave without Ma and Pa and Rebecca. Now that Pa was gone, to and from Leavenworth, Miz Lizbet came downstairs. "It's getting cold up there," she said. She wore her heavy buffalo cape and carried a patchwork bag.

"You're leaving, too?"

"It wouldn't be proper for me to stay here alone with you, Mr. James Weaver."

"Nothing's proper anymore. I don't remember the last time things were proper."

"Well, but I've got business to attend to."

"You can't bring them here while Pa's around, you know."

"It'll soon be too cold for them to travel. I'm heading over to Kentucky, to get some folks ready to steal away in the spring. You won't see me for a long time, Mr. James Weaver, unless they run me off and I've got nowhere else to go."

And then it was like when Will Bowers left and he had nothing to say. "Go in peace, friend," he mumbled.

She slid past James. "And next time you see that rascal Solomon, you tell him not to go getting married, hear?"

CHAPTER TWENTY-SIX

Hog Slaughter

November and December 1856

In his whole life—and he'd be thirteen just after the first of the year—he'd never had such bad food as what he cooked for himself and Pa. His flapjacks were leather patches, and his chicken dribbled a thin stream of pinkish juices, and the lumps in his cornmeal mush were as hard as hailstones. Pa tried not to complain, but James noticed that Pa was pulling his belt a notch tighter.

And then Jeremy came around with the news that it was time to slaughter a few hogs for the winter table. "We're doing our own two, and one for you and one for Olneys', since you *Friends* are too lily-livered to do it yourselves. Come on."

There wasn't anybody to tell he was leaving, so James just took off down the road, with Jeremy babbling about the hog slaughtering. "Once they're dead as a tree stump, we'll boil 'em to loosen the bristles so we can scrape the hide clean. Doesn't tickle, that way."

"I'm not one bit sure I'm going to like this," James said,

hurrying along beside Jeremy. And yet, he was excited at the prospect of doing something so masculinely *Kansas*.

"Oh, you're going to have a picnic. I remember back to my first hog butchering; my pa and I never did have such a good time as that ever again."

They jumped a fence and cut through Barkens' yard. "So then, after the hide's clean, we hang the carcass from a big, thick limb, peel off the hide, gut the thing. There's hardly no waste to a hog. The liver's good, the lungs, the kidneys, the brains. Pigs have got big brains."

"I wouldn't have guessed."

"You like pork sausage?"

"Sure."

Well, Jeremy ruined sausage for him. "It's stuffed into the gut of the hog, you know. We yank out the intestines and scrape 'em, wash 'em good, and fill 'em up with all manner of good savory chopped-up pig meat and spices. Um-*um!*"

What with the food he'd been cooking, and dead-hog talk, James was pretty sure he'd never eat again.

"First thing, we save those good spareribs and backbone. Best eating on the hog. And later on, we'll salt down the shoulders and hams and cure 'em, then we'll hang 'em in the smokehouse for ever and a day, and by Christmas you'll have the tastiest ham you ever put your mouth to."

Well, he sure did love ham, all salty-sweet, lying on a plate next to some hot spiced apples. . . . Maybe this butchering business wouldn't be so bad after all, if it resulted in a fat, pink, juicy Christmas ham.

They jumped the last fence into Macons' place. "Here goes!" Jeremy said, as if he were diving off a cliff.

James hunkered up to sit on the fence for a good view of the whole thing, but Jeremy wouldn't hear of it. "Maybe you ain't gonna kill 'em, but you can sure as the devil help us round 'em up."

With Mr. Macon's help, they chased the four fat porkers out of the barn into a small pen. The hogs looked like they knew what was coming, just like a turkey knows it'll be the guest of honor at dinner soon. So those hogs squealed and caterwauled. James tried to grab one, but it slithered right out of his hands. He was surprised to feel how bristly the hide was—not soft and smooth like a horse.

"Grab one and hang on to him," Mr. Macon yelled, and finally, after about a dozen slip-throughs, James straddled a hog and grabbed its two front legs, the only white parts on the whole black critter. Then, before the hog knew what hit it, Jeremy came down on its head with the handle of an axe. James felt the hog sink out from under his legs.

"Hold his head up," Jeremy commanded, as the butcher knife caught the sun and blinded James while Mr. Macon slit the hog's throat. Blood muddied the ground. James backed away, his stomach heaving.

"Grab another one, James."

But James just kept taking another step back, and another, as Jeremy said to his pa, "What did I do?"

"Aw, nothing, son, there's just different ways of being."

"Bet he'll smack his lips over the spareribs, though."

"Come on, son, we got plenty work to do before we lose the sunlight."

"One man short," Jeremy muttered.

As James slid his leg back over the fence, he suddenly remembered the Hindu man he'd met back in Boston, the only person he ever knew who wasn't a Christian. His skin was nearly as dark as the Negroes' out here. Now, why did he think of that man, all of a sudden, when he'd not given the Hindu a moment's thought in a year's time? And then it hit him—the Hindu was a vegetarian.

After everybody had slaughtered their hogs and here and there a calf, it seemed the typhoid fever spread like grass fire.

"Unsanitary conditions," Dr. Olney said. "Unsanitary meat, unsanitary cooking, unsanitary human hygiene. Sure it's going to spread. Spread like wildfire. Spread like a vicious rumor."

"This isn't the time to talk about such things," said Mrs. Olney, who was trying to hurry them through First Day dinner because her baby was wailing with hunger and clutching at Mrs. Olney's chest right there at the dinner table.

But James was in no hurry to finish this dinner. Real home-cooked food—bread warm from the oven, crusty and brown, but soft as cake inside; sweet potato and pumpkin pie, the color of his own hair; and chicken that wasn't raw a—veritable feast! He ate like he was Moses, starving in the desert for forty days. When he couldn't swallow another bite, and even Pa had to loosen his belt, and the baby could be heard slurping at Mrs. Olney, over in the corner, James went outside to help Solomon groom the horses.

Solomon's arm had healed, but he looked as worn as a rag, because he'd been driving Dr. Olney from house to farm, morning until midnight.

"There's sick people all over this town," he said. They leaned against a bale of prickly hay. The wind whistled through the slats of the barn. Already the water in the trough was starting to freeze up, and the horses needed warm blankets at night and a good rubdown in the morning to get going.

Solomon slyly asked, "Heard from your ma?"

"Not yet. It's only been two weeks."

"Nothing from that other woman, either?" Solomon fiddled with the buckle on his boots.

"Which one's that? Thee means Miz Macon?"

"Other one."

"Dr. Robinson's wife? Miz Bowers? Lots of women around here."

Solomon hung his hat between his knees, just waiting him out.

"Oh, does thee mean Miz Lizbet Charles?"

"That her name?"

"The one who washed thee down like thee was a horse, and put that stinky poultice on thy arm?"

"You're mighty fresh, James Weaver."

"Her? Naw, I haven't heard from her," he said, stealing a sideways glance at Solomon. "Oh, except she gave me a message for thee. Something about getting married."

Solomon tossed his hat in the air, and it landed on a horse's head. "Miz Lizbet's fixin' to get married?"

"Did I say that?" James turned to the horse that was trying to buck off the hat. "Did I tell the man she was getting married?" The horse whinnied. "I believe the message was more like, 'You tell that Solomon not to run off and marry anybody.'"

Solomon's weary face lit up.

"Thee watch out for her when she comes back in the spring. I think she likes thee, Solomon."

Maybe because he was still so weak from his journey, or maybe because he'd been to so many sick houses, Solomon came down with the typhoid fever. James and Pa ran into Dr. Olney at Round Corner Drug Store, and the doctor said, "Caleb, I can't risk his giving it to my little one, if she's going to make it through her first winter out here." In a few short months, James was already taller than Dr. Olney, who was looking thin, his cheeks all sunken, his face grayish.

Pa said, "Thee must bring Solomon to our house."

What? Who would take care of him?

"It's just James and me, and we're of hearty stock." Dr. Olney nodded; there was no time for flowery thank-you's.

Pa had to go over to Lecompton to pick up some legal papers, but he swore he'd be home before dark to help look after Solomon.

Solomon came to the house, leaning heavily on little Dr. Olney. "Where to?" the doctor asked.

"There's a small room upstairs," James said. *Miz Lizbet's room.*

"He needs a warm place. Fix him a pallet in front of

the fire." James ran upstairs and dragged the straw mattress and a couple of bedsheets down. Solomon slumped in the rocker, while Dr. Olney rolled his sleeves up. "Where's your pa?"

"He'll be back by nightfall. Promised."

They quickly made up a bed for Solomon on the floor. His knees buckled and he nearly collapsed on the bed. James drew the top sheet up to Solomon's chin.

"More blankets," Dr. Olney said. "He'll have the shakes in a minute, and just when thee's got him warmed up, he'll kick off all the covers with the sweats. Thee will have thy hands full, son."

So, in barely the time for the crack of a whip, James became not only a bad cook, but also a bad nurse. Dr. Olney told him everything he needed to know, while Solomon snored loudly. "The poor man will have pains in his head, his back, his arms and legs. Nothing to do for it. He may vomit."

"I couldn't handle that, Dr. Olney."

The doctor glared at him, while he rolled his sleeves down again. "Thee can handle whatever thee has to, friend."

"Yes sir."

"Advanced stages, he'll have ulcerations in his intestines."

"Ulcerations, sir?"

"Open sores, inside. Very painful. Just try to keep him comfortable."

"Snug as a bug in a rug," James said.

"My words exactly. And wash him with cool water for the fever, give him lots to drink, clear liquids, not milk, and thee must be sure to wash thine own hands real carefully after thee takes care of Solomon. And pray he's strong enough to make it through, in spite of thy care."

James shot nervous glances toward Solomon, who seemed to be drifting in and out of sleep. "I sure wish my ma was back from Boston."

"Well, I wish I was *there,* son. People don't die of typhoid in Boston." Dr. Olney slipped on his coat. And soon it was just James and a sick-to-dying man alone in this house, with the first snow of the winter bunching up on the windows.

It was going to be a long winter.

Dark, and there was no sign of Pa. Solomon moaned, sort of sucked his lips like a fish.

"Thee must be thirsty." James put a dipper of water to Solomon's lips, but the man hadn't the strength to sit up. He remembered how Miz Lizbet and Ma had spooned water into Rebecca's mouth, and so he tried doing the same thing. Most of the water slid down Solomon's chin. He tilted his head back to let the water cool his feverish neck. James needed to wash him down, but he'd never done such a thing and couldn't imagine touching another person so intimately. But he went for a pan of water and hoped he could just hand the damp rag to Solomon to do the business himself. And what if Solomon had to relieve himself? He thought about Henry Brown, the man who mailed himself in a packing crate, and Rebecca's asking what he did when he had to make water while he was going through the mail. If only Miz Lizbet had told them that night!

Suddenly the door burst open, as if the wind had forced the catch, and there was a vicious blast of cold air. Solomon's eyes grew terrified at the sudden shift in temperature. James got up to close the door—and saw her standing there.

"Miz Lizbet!" His first thought was, *she's here to help with Solomon.* But one look at her, and he realized he'd have two patients on his hands. And then it struck him that Pa would be back before the night was out, and he'd catch Miz Lizbet, and when Ma got back, James would be to blame for it all.

Miz Lizbet fell onto the mattress in front of the fire, as if there weren't already an occupant there. She simply shoved Solomon over. She was wheezing, trying to catch her breath so she could speak.

"You can't stay. Pa's due back any minute." He heard the terrible rattling in her chest. She motioned for something to drink, and he fetched her a cup of water, hot off the stove. She looked awful, with dark rings under her eyes. Her buffalo cape slid down to reveal spindles of hair, and welts on her neck.

Oh Lord.

Solomon woke up, surprised to find he wasn't alone. "Mizlizbet?"

Finally, she caught her voice and asked, "What's he doing here?"

"Typhoid fever," James said.

She felt his face, which was the color of burnished copper. "Burning up."

"Can thee do anything?" James asked helplessly.

"Of course, soon as I can breathe."

161

"But thee can't stay—"

"Don't be foolish. It's down way below freezing out there. Your daddy can't get through in this weather, and I sure can't go back out in it. I told you I'd only come back if I had nowhere else to go." She was starting to warm up, so she slipped the cape off. "I need help pulling off my boots, because my fingers are frozen and they might just snap off if I pull too hard."

So James yanked at her boots, and with them came the rags her feet had been wrapped in. Her bare feet embarrassed him—so pink on the bottom, but the toenails were pitch-black from the boots. Or was it gangrene? She sipped at the hot water and also dabbed at Solomon's neck with the washrag. "I've had days I liked better than this one," she said. "Solomon Jefferson, you're going to have to sit up so's I can take your shirt off, or you're going to be delirious with fever in a minute."

And then, she seemed to take over as usual, ordering James around to fetch this and that. "More blankets. I'll make me a bed here beside Solomon. We won't neither one of us sleep much tonight, anyway."

James was sure that he'd never in his life been so glad to see anyone as he was to see Miz Lizbet, no matter what kind of a fit Pa would have when he came home. If Pa made it through what was becoming not just the first snowfall, but the first blizzard of the winter.

CHAPTER TWENTY-SEVEN

The Funeral

It was one of the wettest summers in Kansas history—the kind they could have used back in the 1850s or 1930s. But the farmers who'd begged for water in the spring were now bailing it out of their wheat fields before the harvest rotted.

Dr. Baxi, the coroner, came in out of an energetic storm to give Dana and her family the final results of his study on Lizbet Charles. Dana's mother took his raincoat and hung it over the bathtub, and Dr. Baxi sat in the front room in his stocking feet while his boots dried. "How's Save Wolcott Castle coming, Jeffrey?"

"We're hoping to raise $100,000 at the July Fourth party. We'll either have a thousand people there, or twenty-five. Could go either way. I'd gladly hit you up for a donation, but I'm sure you're here for another reason."

"Yes, the remains."

So, Lizbet Charles was reduced to the status of "remains"? How demoralizing! He wouldn't feel that way when she gave him the journal, Dana thought.

"It's generous of you to share the results with us, Punir," her mother said.

"Dana found the subject, and she was there at the initial examination. I thought you all might like to know what we've confirmed before the report is released to the press tomorrow."

Raindrops came down the chimney and splattered on the fireplace grate, as Dr. Baxi began his explanation. "We've ground up bone fragments, put them in a liquid solution, and run them through the gas chromatograph and mass spectrometer."

His accent made it difficult for Dana to figure out just what these technological wonders really were, but she said, "Sounds impressive. I guess you learned a lot?"

"Not so much," he said sadly. "We know the subject wasn't poisoned, nor did she die of any sort of drug ingestion."

Dana's mother said, "Aren't we relieved to know she wasn't a junkie, 135 years ago?"

"Also," Dr. Baxi continued, "we know she died in the winter, because very cold conditions would retard putrefaction, and there were actually patches of tissue internally protected by the large-mass bones. I surmise that the cold weather preserved her somewhat, and that there followed a very dry spring that partially mummified the remains."

Lizbet Charles was a mummy? Didn't they go out of style in King Tut's time?

Dana's father asked, "Then, what did she die of?"

"Well, it is more productive to say what she *didn't* die of. There is no evidence of a gunshot wound, no place where a knife penetrated bone, or a blunt object cracked bone. Obviously, there was no fire in the room."

"Couldn't she have died in a fire first, and then been dragged into the room?" asked Dana.

Dr. Baxi stroked his chin. "Possible, but not likely. Judging by the arrangement of the bones, she died in that bed. And I submit that she wasn't in a raging fire *anywhere,* because her bones are in good condition. You know, it's not unusual for a skull to literally burst outward from the intensity of heat in a fire."

"Oh, that's terrible," Dana's mother cried.

"Nor could we prove smoke inhalation, without lung tissue to examine."

Dana's father said, "But she *could* have died of smoke inhalation, maybe during Quantrill's raid on Lawrence in 1863?"

Dr. Baxi shook his head. "Simon Fleicher, the forensic anthropologist, places her death between 1855 and 1860, definitely pre–Civil War. But when his graduate students studied the climatic conditions of the period, they found the year I was looking for in terms of her degree of preservation, that is, an intensely cold winter, followed by a very dry spring. I say she died in the winter of 1856."

Dana was getting confused with all the technological detail, and she just wanted the bottom line. "Well then, how *did* she die?"

"Natural causes."

"What? How boring," her mother said, but then she added, "The poor thing was only about twenty years old; why would she die of natural causes?"

"I don't necessarily mean heart degeneration or any such thing. It is my hypothesis that she died of the natural progression of a disease, such as cholera. The grad students suggest this as a possibility, although the cholera epidemic passed through here about ten years before the subject died. Malaria's another possibility, or yellow fever, smallpox, even simple pneumonia. These were not easy times in your country."

Dana thought about Millicent Weaver's saying, "These are troubling times," and worrying that she'd never get back to see Caleb or James again. Did she?

"But it sounds like you have a different theory, Punir. Care to share it?"

"Hypothesis, you understand, Jeffrey. I am sticking my neck out, but it's a very short neck. Still, based on the research of the period, I'd submit that the young lady died of typhoid fever."

Just what Jeep said! "Before or after she got to the room?"

"I say she died in the room, but now you're talking speculation," Dr. Baxi said thoughtfully. "Or conjecture, whichever you prefer."

But what else did they have? They couldn't take a giant leap back in history and live out Lizbet's last days. Dana called Mike and Derek, Sally and Ahn, and, of course, Jeep. "I'm cancelling the pact," she told each of them. "Lizbet Charles is back, and we're putting her to rest."

166

Just after dinner, they met outside Lizbet's room. Dana said, "This is her funeral."

"Funeral? Then we need some good sappy music," said Derek.

"No, just our voices," Dana decided. She knew how she wanted to do this, and they were just going to have to go along with it all, or she'd do it alone. She led them past the barricades into the little room where Lizbet had spent her last hours. She put a candle in the center of the room and sat down on the rough floor. They all solemnly followed. Holding hands, they formed a tight circle, and the only light was the candlelight, which made the corners of the small room seem like nests of secrets.

And they talked about everyone they'd ever cared about who'd died.

Mike: "When I was three, my turtle Shellshock . . ."

Sally: "My great-grandmother was so old she couldn't even . . ."

Derek: "Jim Morrison drugged himself to death. Idiotic . . ."

Ahn: "My parents, both the same night . . ."

Dana: "President Kennedy . . ."

Jeep: "Miz Lizbet Charles."

CHAPTER TWENTY-EIGHT

The Return of Marshal Fain

December 1856

James brought in all the firewood and stacked it along the back wall, before the snow drifted so high that they couldn't open the door. Snow covered the ice on the windows. It was eerie not to be able to see out, even in broad daylight. They were cut off, sealed in, but inside it was warm, and Miz Lizbet looked after James and Solomon, and there was a feeling of making do, like camping by a river, and it wasn't so bad.

Two days passed before the storm stopped raging enough for James to shovel a path to their door, in case Pa was trying to get home. Trembles wouldn't even poke his head out the door.

Solomon grew stronger and was sitting up at the table after four days of Miz Lizbet's care and cooking. James had just scooped himself up some rabbit stew—his vegetarian days had passed quickly—when he heard the crunching of boots on the snow.

James opened the door on a glorious day, deceptively sunny, but still bitter cold, and there came Pa up the front steps. James rushed up to him, but stopped just short of throwing his arms around him.

"Lord it's good to see thee, son!" Pa pulled him close. Everything about him was cold—his rough coat, his rough beard, which James had thought he might never feel against his skin again. And then he was gripped with the horrifying thought: *Miz Lizbet.*

"Good day, Mr. Weaver," Miz Lizbet said, while she fed Solomon spoonfuls of her chicken broth. Solomon lifted his heavy head and managed a weak, "Welcome home, Mr. Weaver."

Pa looked them both over, was silent for a good long minute while he prayed and thought it through, and finally he said, "Thee's been most helpful."

"That's true, Mr. Weaver, because Solomon needed more than the boy could provide, and I suspect you could use a good hot meal yourself." She hurried to the stove to ladle out some stew for Pa.

"Thank thee kindly," Pa said, while James paced the room searching for some way to explain just who Miz Lizbet was.

Pa yanked his boots off and kneeled on Solomon's bed, warming his hands over the fire. Miz Lizbet stood behind him, with the dinner plate in her hand.

"I trust you're Mrs. Weaver's handiwork?" he asked.

"Yes sir."

Pa sighed.

169

"But it's not her fault, Mr. Weaver, or your boy James's, either. I just kept coming back and wouldn't leave."

Pa slid his hands back and forth until his dry skin made a near-screeching sound. Miz Lizbet, Solomon, James—all of them held their breath, until Pa said, "Thee's welcome here."

James was giddy with relief. "Her name's Lizbet Charles, Pa. We didn't mean to keep it from thee, honest, we just—"

Pa waved his words away. "Thy mother is a resolute woman. The day we married, she swore to love and honor, but not to obey." Pa got to his feet and took the dinner plate from Miz Lizbet. He fingered a bit of butter off the top of the corn bread before it all melted in. He put his plate down and straddled a chair across from Solomon, while they all waited. "But we shall have to be discreet, Miz Lizbet Charles. Now, have thee said grace?"

By the tenth of December, the snow was packed into thick bales in the drifts, but the roads were fairly clear for travel—and brought Marshal Fain back. It was just luck that Miz Lizbet was down in the cellar when he arrived, and had the good sense to stay there when she heard voices.

Marshal Fain stood in the doorway, waiting to be asked in. No one asked. Trembles arched his back and stared the marshal down. Finally, Pa said, "Well, it's cold. Thee might at least close the door behind thee. What brings thee here?"

"Just checking to see how you weathered the storm, Mr. Weaver."

"Well as to be expected."

Marshal Fain looked around the room, inspecting. "The wife back yet?"

"We expect her as soon as the weather clears up."

The marshal tapped the toe of his boot on the floor, until Pa had no choice but to direct him to sit down. Solomon quickly left the table, knowing the marshal wouldn't sit there with him.

"Who's this, Mr. Weaver?"

"Now, thee knows who this is, Mr. Fain. Don't toy with us."

The marshal squinted toward Solomon. "I don't believe I've seen this individual before."

"Yes sir, you have, Marshal, last time you were here," James said. "You studied his papers. He's Solomon Jefferson, a free man, remember?"

"Well now, I make a lot of stops on my circuit. Could be I remember, could be I don't. You got those papers with you, boy?"

"No sir," Solomon said, his jaws clenched.

Marshal Fain looked around the room. "It's looking mighty orderly for a place where three men's holed up in the winter. Hot pot of coffee on the stove, a pot of something tangy steaming. Sure smells good."

"My son James has become quite a cook since his mother's been gone," Pa said, with a twinkle in his eye. James smiled to himself, then took the cue and lifted the lid on the pot boiling on the stove, swirled the stringy gray stuff around with Ma's big pewter ladle.

"About done," James said, though it might have needed forty more hours to cook, for all he knew.

171

"Nice lacy doilies on the table. Sure looks like a woman's touch," said Marshal Fain.

"Thee might get to the point, friend."

"Well, Mr. Weaver, folks say there's a Nigra woman in and out of here. Folks saw her come in not long ago, never saw her go out."

James stole a glance at Solomon, and both of them stood frozen in place.

Pa stood up and loomed over the marshal. "I have no use for thy accusations, sir, and I would appreciate thy vacating my home." Pa's voice was calm, but James read the anger soaring through him.

Marshal Fain just crossed his ankle over his knee, as if he planned to stay a good long while.

What would Will's pa or Jeremy's pa do at a time like this? Probably chase the marshal with a gun, fire at his toes while he hotfooted it down the front steps.

"I do not lose my temper easily," Pa said, "but thee is provoking me." Pa snatched off the marshal's hat, with the showy badge on it. "A gentleman takes off his hat indoors, sir." He threw the hat down on the chair and sat on it.

James could barely keep from laughing, especially when he thought of the joke that used to go around the Meeting House in Boston. A burglar breaks into a Friend's house, and the pa catches the burglar red-handed. He grabs a hunting rifle and aims it at the man. Well, the burglar's not expecting this, says, "You don't scare me a bit. I know a Quaker would never shoot a man." And the pa replies, "I have no intention of harming thee, friend, but thee's standing where I aim to shoot."

James was remembering how all the men and boys used to laugh over this joke, when Marshal Fain turned pure mean.

"I am warning you, Caleb Weaver, I'll get you for hiding runaway Nigras. All I need's proof, and I'll get that. My men will be watching here night and day, and we'll arrest you *and* any darkie that goes in or out your door. In or out, Mr. Caleb Weaver, night or day, you hear?" He got up abruptly and strode to the door.

Outside, James spotted a posse of the meanest, dirtiest-looking Border Ruffians, sporting no telling what kind of guns, and all of them blowing into their hands to keep warm.

These were the kinds of men Will Bowers was out hunting down.

CHAPTER TWENTY-NINE

Up to the Tower

With Lizbet Charles officially dead again and laid to rest, and the journal in Dr. Baxi's hands, there was only one thing Dana still needed to do. She *had* to get into the house that James Weaver built.

"You've got a key to Wolcott Castle, Dad, why won't you let me in?"

"Because the place is a death trap. Why do you think it's going to take a quarter of a million dollars to restore it? You can poke your finger through the walls where the termites have feasted, and the floors collapse with the slightest pressure. There's broken glass all around, and one more windstorm will send the roof flying to Nebraska. Flat-out no!"

Which, of course, meant yes to Dana. There had to be a way.

"Simple," Jeep said. "I climb that giant elm out there and catapult myself onto the second-floor flat roof."

"And then what?" Ahn asked.

"Well, then it's so easy my little brothers could do it. All the windows up there are broken out. You just find a jagged hole big enough to crawl through."

Ahn cried, "I don't want to be shredded."

"Don't you ever watch cop shows? I'll just stick my hand in and unlock the window and push it up."

Dana said, "So, let me see if I've got this. You're going to do all that, and then you're going to come downstairs and open the front door for us poor helpless girls?"

"Well, yeah, that'll work."

"No way. I'm the one who's going in through the window."

"We all go in through the window," Ahn said, with a sigh.

Jeep grinned. "Just name the night."

Friday. That gave Dana three days to gather supplies and plan the strategy, including what to tell her parents if they all fell through the floor and died.

On Friday, Dr. Baxi phoned.

"Dana? Thank you for giving us the journal—finally. We have all read it, the police and Dr. Fleicher and myself. Very interesting. But I'm afraid it's not too useful in closing the case. There are still too many unraveling ends. Now, what to do with the journal?"

Ahn and Jeep were arguing over what food to bring on the break-in. "Shh!" Dana hissed, covering the mouthpiece of the phone.

175

"We have decided to give the journal to the Douglas County Historical Society."

Dana's heart sank. It was *hers*!

"The curator at the museum has promised that it will be exhibited as a gift from Dana Shannon. Very nice."

Well, better than nothing.

By the end of the call, Ahn had everything—including a bag of potato chips and some onion dip—stuffed in a backpack, and now they only had to wait for nine o'clock when it would be dark enough to walk over to Vermont Avenue for their first breaking and entering into a castle.

As a big concession to his male ego, Dana let Jeep wear the backpack as they scrambled up the tree. But she was the first one to leap across space to the second-story overhang.

They found the window with the biggest hole and least number of jagged edges, and they stuffed Ahn through it, so she could open another window from the inside. And then they were in a room covered with empty book-shelves and cobwebs worthy of a Halloween spook house.

The floor seemed squishy, and the walls yielded like cardboard sets in a play. Something flew by. "What was that?"

"Don't ask." Dana led the way. A huge white thing gleamed down the hall—an ancient bathtub that hulked along the bathroom wall on dragon's claws, like a beast ready to strike.

Ahn gasped. "Why did I listen to you guys?"

"What are we supposed to be looking for?" asked Jeep.

"I don't know—James-isms. Something that tells us what kind of a guy he grew up to be."

"Well, we have to go up to the tower." Jeep swept his flashlight over the rounded walls of the main hall. Waist down, the walls were some dark kind of wood, and up to the ceiling, they were all peeling plaster and chipped paint. Two sconces that had once probably held kerosene lamps hung by a thread.

"Nice place here," Ahn said, as something furry with very short legs and a long pointy tail scurried past them.

Finally, Jeep spotted a child-sized door open an inch or two. He yanked at the bloated wood, and the door creaked open just enough for them to slip into the stair-well. The stairs wound and wound upward, only wide enough for one person at a time.

"Ladies first."

"Not me," Ahn said, but Jeep reassured her. "Keep going. I'm right behind you."

The room at the top was so narrow that if you stood in the center and stretched out your arms, you could put your palm flat on each side.

"Hey, I'm holding up the tower," Jeep bragged.

The red brick walls had tiny gold stars painted on them, and moons, and Saturn and comets and Jupiter. An ancient telescope stood with its eye to a window.

"That's to find the North Star," Ahn whispered. "Well, this has been nice. Ready to go down?" She eagerly led the way back to the stairs, but one glance down into the dark pit of the stairwell and she begged, "Just toss me out the tower window." But she followed Dana down the stairs, all of them in a tight chain.

"What smells so ripe and musty?" Dana asked.

Jeep knew. "Bat guano. Haven't you ever been in a cave?"

"Bats?!"

"Quiet, you'll scare the roaches."

"That's it, I'm getting out of here," Ahn said.

"Weren't you the one who wasn't even scared at *A Nightmare on Elm Street*?" asked Jeep.

"Yes, but this is real life. I'll wait out on the front porch. Don't leave without me." And she rushed down the stairs, slamming the front door on her way out.

Dana and Jeep crept carefully into a massive room that faced the rear of the house. Maybe it was once Edmund Wolcott's bedroom. Dana imagined a huge four-poster bed with red drapes and a satin footstool, which Edmund, the cattle baron, must have used to mount his bed.

Jeep whistled. "Check out this window." It was about twelve feet high, floor to ceiling, swinging open like a door, and beyond was a small balcony. Jeep left the backpack in Edmund's room, and they stepped onto the balcony, sucking up the welcome breeze after the stifling, dank house.

Then, in a second, Jeep vanished, as if he'd fallen through a trapdoor. Something—probably his flashlight—dropped and shattered way below him.

Dana's flashlight darted around. There was no sign of Jeep, except for his hollering— "Ahhhhhhhhhhh!"—

until she saw the tips of his fingers, bloodless white, clinging to the top side of the rotten floorboard. Jeep hung below, his feet thrashing around for something to glom on to. But there was nothing except deep space.

"Hang on, Jeep!"

"No other choice." His words came in short bursts.

The thing was to distribute her weight evenly so the rest of the balcony wouldn't collapse. She lay herself carefully across what remained of the balcony floor and thrust her hands down into the darkness. "Can you see my hands?"

"Sure, so what? You think I'm gonna let go of these boards?"

"Wait, I'll shine the flashlight down below you."

"Ahh, not in my eyes!"

"Right. I'm going to see if there's something soft you can jump down to."

Three floors below and sunk deep into the ground was an empty swimming pool. And that's if he could slide like a missile through space, straight down. If he missed by a foot or two, he'd land on a wrought-iron fence that had lethal-looking keep-out points on it. "Hey, Jeep, don't look down, and don't jump. I'll pull you up."

"Fast. My arms are getting awful long."

"Give me one hand. You hold on to the boards with the other one, just in case."

Dana plunged her hands down into the dark hole, grabbing one of Jeep's wrists. But he weighed a lot more than she did, and it was hard to get any leverage, lying flat on her belly. She used her elbows, as if she were arm wrestling, but she wasn't strong enough to lift him straight up. If she could wrap his hand around one of those sturdy posts . . . "Don't let go of me!"

"You kiddin'?"

She reached for a low post on the balcony railing— and it broke off in her hand. But it was rounded on one side, flat on the other. Idea! "Okay, Jeep, listen up. I've got this thick piece of wood here. I'm going to lay it across the hole, and I'm going to support it with all my weight on both ends—somehow. When I say *now,* grab it and see if you can chin yourself up on it."

She straddled the post and willed herself to be worth at least 200 pounds. "Now!"

Jeep grunted with his effort, but finally she saw the top of his head. Bending from the waist, still supporting both ends of the post with her feet, she reached down and grabbed Jeep around the neck.

He came up like a jack-in-the-box. "You're choking me."

"Well, you'd be dead if I weren't."

Now she had a good grip on his throat, so she could get off the post and give him a hearty yank until he bent his chest over the balcony floor.

He lay across the floor, coughing and gasping for breath.

"You okay?"

"Sure," he said faintly.

They crawled back into Edmund's bedroom and leaned against a wall. Assorted vermin scuttled across their feet, but it didn't matter much anymore.

Finally, Dana said, "What are we doing tomorrow night? Skydiving?"

"This James guy, he didn't do such an outstanding job in designing balconies."

"It's not his fault," Dana said. "It's time and weather." She rummaged around in the backpack, found the potato chips. "Want some?"

"Leave 'em for the rats," Jeep muttered.

"What a guy."

"It's true, I am."

"No, I meant James Weaver," Dana teased, her mouth full of ranch-flavored chips.

CHAPTER THIRTY

Amen

December 1856

A few scrawny blackbirds fluttered past the window. It was getting to be nearly Christmas, and there was no sign of Ma and Rebecca. Jeremy Macon brought one letter out from town, though.

December 12, 1856

Dear Ones,

My father has passed on to the next world. Mother kept him four days in the parlor until the snow lessened enough that we could lay him to rest in the Boston soil he dearly loved.

Rebecca and I shall head home just as soon as weather permits, although it's madness to travel in the ruin of winter. But we cannot bear to be away from thee on Christmas. Too much time has passed already.

Keep our faces in thy mind's eye, and our safe return in thy prayers.

Pa read the letter aloud, emphasizing this part or that each time he read it. "Father Baylor gone. Four days, bless his soul. They'll be heading home! Too much time indeed."

James couldn't imagine a world in which he'd never see Grampa Baylor again. Sure, a man's soul passed into eternity, but still, death was so unfair. Where was the justice in not having a grandfather to talk to? Grampa Weaver had died before James could even talk, and now with Grampa Baylor gone, he felt so . . . silenced. He thought of the sketch he'd done of Grampa's dog Timbre.

"Why, it's the very likeness! Thee is a true craftsman."

"Naw, Grampa, it's just a little old ink drawing. See here, the ears are too floppy, and I didn't get the eyes just right. Timbre's eyes, they laugh; here they don't."

Grampa had picked up his walking stick, fancy with delicate carvings of the Greek gods, and poked it in James's ribs. "James, thee must look at the work of thy hands as a gift God has planted within thee, and thee must honor it by letting the gift pass through thy fingers."

"But I can't do it right."

Poke, deep into his belly. "Does thee not think Michelangelo had a critical eye for his statues and paintings? And yet, see how they stand today." He'd miraculously plucked the right book off his shelf of thousands of books and laid it open to a picture Michelangelo had painted up on the ceiling of some church in Rome, Italy.

Breathtaking, impossible! "I'm no Michelangelo," James had said, humbly looking at his feet but thinking, *maybe I just might be!*

"No sir, thee is not a Michelangelo. Thee is a James Baylor Weaver. And I swear, I shall carry thy sketch of Timbre to my grave."

No one else had heard this conversation, and surely no one had thought to slip that old sketch in Grampa Baylor's suit pocket before the coffin lid slammed shut. And now he was six feet under, and James was 1,500 miles away from him, and there was just no absolute guarantee, out here in this wilderness, that spring would ever come.

Solomon peeked down over the railing of the steps. "Mr. Weaver, sir, Miz Lizbet's taken sick."

On the first clear day, Pa brushed past the two guards who camped outside their house in a buffalo-hide tent, cooking over an open fire, huddling under blankets to keep from freezing. Their sitting out there was pure stupidity, but it seemed that Marshal Fain was determined.

"Where you goin'?" one of them asked.

"To a quilting bee," Pa said snidely.

"Trying to slip a Nigra past us?"

"No sir, trying to get into town to see if there's any word from my wife, and to buy a cot for the man who's stopping with us."

"That nigger?" The man's nose was blue, would probably be frostbitten right off before long—at least James hoped so.

"No sir, for the free man who's been helping us out while my wife's been gone to Boston. Say, it's nice and warm inside there, gentlemen. Pity thee can't come in and have some hot spiced cider beside the fire."

James saw the two men stir and exchange longing glances.

"But the marshal wouldn't like it now, would he?"

They put the second cot beside Miz Lizbet's, upstairs in the little room. She tossed about, and that rudely crafted cot clunked against the floor as it rose and fell with her restlessness. Solomon filled bladders with boiling water to warm her bed. He ran up and down the stairs with panfuls of heated rocks for a cairn. The stones sizzled when he tossed water on them to make steam for Miz Lizbet's comfort. He sat in the rocker beside her bed, wrapped in blankets and skins, and they said little.

James came upstairs every so often with fresh rocks, or a bit of soup for Miz Lizbet. He overheard her say, "They'll be waiting for you over in Kentucky, just after the first thaw. They're ready to make free, Solomon, and I won't be able to go after them."

"Hush, Lizbet. In the spring we'll go after them together."

"In the spring, I'll be in the dirt."

"In the spring, you'll be my wife. We're gonna have beautiful, smart children, free children."

James's face was hot with shame for overhearing their private cooings. He turned around and went back downstairs.

Later that day, when James came up to check on Miz

Lizbet, she said, "Solomon, you go get some rest, and let me talk to Mr. James Weaver a minute, hear?"

Solomon reluctantly backed out of the little room, stooping to clear the doorway.

"James Weaver, listen fast, because I haven't got much gumption."

James pulled the rocking chair up close.

"Your mother's a saint, but the rest of you aren't so bad, come to find out."

"Thee's given us fits, Miz Lizbet."

She nodded, with great effort. "Meant to. Now, run your hand under this bed and see if you can find something."

James slapped around on the floorboards until he found a small black book. "Is this what thee means?"

Miz Lizbet nodded wearily. "Your mother's. She taught me to read, but I never learned to read well enough to get through this. You take it."

"I couldn't."

"Why are you always so contrary, Mr. James Weaver?"

"Miz Lizbet, I know my ma about as well as anybody does. If she gave this to thee, she meant for thee to have it." He slipped it into Miz Lizbet's hands.

Her eyes fluttered closed. He expected to hear "Amen," but she was too weak to say the word.

They sent for Dr. Olney, telling the guards outside that James had broken his arm. Then he had to walk around with it in a sling all the time because those evil men were forever peering in the windows, trying to entrap them— or maybe just soaking up some warmth with their eyes.

On the fifth night, when Miz Lizbet's fever still hadn't broken, James and Pa had a heart-to-heart about their choices.

"What happens if they get us, Pa?"

"Well, most likely they'll haul me off to jail. I don't think they'd touch thee, thee being but a child."

"Jail. Oh Pa. And there's not another lawyer around to defend thee."

"I'd live through it. That's not what worries me, son. It's them." He raised his eyebrows, motioning to the people upstairs. "Solomon would probably be safe, since he's got legal papers, if that marshal's got a shred of honor and respect for the law."

"And Miz Lizbet?"

"No telling. They're probably looking for her, son, since she's helped so many shed the chains of bondage."

"You mean, sick as she is, they might still drag her down to where she came from and try to sell her back?"

"They'd do worse, son."

"And if she dies?"

"Dead, she's worth even more to them."

"We don't have any choices, then."

"Best thy mother doesn't come back to this mess," Pa said sadly.

"What do we do, Pa?" His pa gave him a good, steady look. Maybe he saw that James wasn't such a boy anymore, that his shoulders were broadening and his flanks were thinning out.

"All through thy life, son, I've made decisions for thee. Thee hasn't liked them all."

"No sir." James smiled.

Pa went over to the fireplace and stabbed at a log. Red jewels sprang forth. "Thee must make this choice, son."

"Me?" Choose to send Pa to jail, or Miz Lizbet to death, or worse?

"The Lord gives thee free will."

Free will. He would run down to Macons', bring back a revolver, yes! When those men were frozen to distraction, looking covetously at the smoke rising from the chimney, James could steal up behind them, shoot 'em in cold blood. It's what Will Bowers would do, heck, what Will was probably doing this very minute.

Then Solomon could take Miz Lizbet somewhere safe, maybe to the Olneys', until she got well. And Pa would be safe, and Ma, and Rebecca. He'd get caught, of course, but wasn't it a sacrifice any man would make for those he loved?

"Has thee chosen, son?"

James pictured the dead men, the snow colored with their blood, pink as strawberry ice. He could bury them under a drift; no one would find them until the spring thaw. By then all the Weavers could be safely back in Boston. So reasonable. So easy.

"Son?"

"We stay right here and outwait 'em. We're a peaceable people, Pa."

"Yes, son."

The next time James went upstairs with heated rocks, Solomon didn't even turn around. He swayed in the rocker, his back to James, and said, "She's passed."

"Pa! Come quick." What were they to do now?

188

But Pa had it all thought out. "There's a cache of lumber down in the cellar, left when Mr. Madison rebuilt our house. Bring it here, nails, too."

Trip after trip, James hauled the lumber upstairs with one arm in a sling, while Solomon washed Miz Lizbet once more, for her final journey home.

The three of them stood around her bed, and Pa read from Psalms, from Lamentations, from Genesis: "'Wherefore didst thou flee away secretly, and steal away from me; and didst not tell me, that I might have sent thee away with mirth. . . .'"

James thought of Henry Box Brown, and Miz Ellen Craft dressed up like a gentleman planter, and Uncle Mose riding off triumphantly, and all the other Negroes who'd made it to freedom. And of Matthew Luke Charles, who didn't. Then he thought about the fish fry outside, and the smelly poultice of prairie clover and the wild indigo tea, and Miz Lizbet struggling to write her *G*s at Ma's table.

Dimly, he heard Pa's voice. "Lord, we entrust Miss Elizabeth Charles into Thy hands and pray that Thou grantest her the eternal rest she's earned."

Pa took the rocking chair and the cairn out of the room. Solomon pulled a thin sheet up over Miz Lizbet's head, and they set to building the wall.

CHAPTER THIRTY-ONE

Written in Stone

The governor and a few other dignitaries had chairs reserved inside the tent, but most of the six hundred people on the grounds of Wolcott Castle had paid from $100 to $1,000 to broil in the July Fourth sun.

Dana and Ahn and Jeep got into the party free, because they'd licked about four thousand envelopes and stamps.

Ahn surveyed the enormous stone front. "It looks better from the outside, and not so scary in the daylight."

Dana said, "It seems more like James Weaver from the outside."

"The *old* James Weaver," Ahn said.

"Well, he was only thirty-three when he built it."

"Yes," said Ahn, "but somehow I thought he'd always be our age."

A young couple walked by them, holding hands. The

guy, who must have been sweltering in a suit and tie, said, "I'd sure like to see the inside."

"No, you wouldn't," Jeep muttered under his breath.

The woman replied dreamily, "Let's have balconies like those when we build our house. They're so romantic, aren't they, honey?"

"Try hanging from one, lady," Jeep whispered.

Dana laughed and sipped a frosty glass of iced tea, as her father's voice bombarded the crowd, thanks to the free services of Sensory Sound of Lawrence.

"Ladies and gentlemen, in a minute we'll hear from the honorable Jacqueline Marx, governor of the state of Kansas. But first, I'd like to welcome . . ."

"Whew, it's hot," Jeep said. "Let's sit under this tree here that looks like somebody could climb it and swing onto the house from it, if somebody was a maniac lunatic crazy person." He plunked himself down under the giant elm, expecting the soft earth to yield to him. Instead, he got a jolt up his spine. "What's this?" Jeep clawed away the tall grass, and underneath, embedded in the earth, was a granite plaque, like a flat gravestone.

"Somebody is buried here?" Ahn asked.

"I dunno, I can't read it." Jeep continued to clear the grass away.

Dana slid closer, just as the crowd was welcoming Governor Marx. The words on the marker were impossible to read, because layers of dirt clogged the carved letters, and half the marker was still buried under tree roots and grass. Dana poured her iced tea over the stone and wiped away rivulets of dirt with a napkin, while Jeep yanked at the exposed roots.

191

They could make out the first few words now: "Buildings crumble."

"Get some more tea," Dana whispered.

The governor's musical voice went up and down the scale: "Today the good people of Lawrence, Kansas, have pledged to restore this monument to their proud history. . . ."

Jeep and Ahn came back, each with two full glasses of iced tea and a pile of napkins. They doused the stone, washing away the dirt until at last everything was clear.

Buildings crumble,
but leaves and grass are eternal.
I plant this tree in memory of
MATTHEW LUKE CHARLES
and
ELIZABETH CHARLES
April 20, 1877
J. B. W./amen